Praise for *The Cu*

"Creative, lyrical, whacky, ..., and sad all at once. Andrew Brush presents the juxtaposition of farcical and morbid elements with disturbing effect. A great read."
**-The Telegraph, Lifestyle journalist, Eleanore Kelly**

"Hunter S. Thompson's bastard offspring is living in Cheltenhamshire, and his name is Andrew Brush. Quite brilliant."
**-Cotswold Life: Candia McKormack, Editor**

"Beautifully poetic and melancholic, with razor sharp wit and a touch of the absurd. An utterly original book."
**-Sunday Express: Victoria Grey (Group Lifestyle Editor Mirror/Express supplements, OK! and New magazine)**

"Quickfire and intricate – a true original."
**-GQ: Thomas Barrie, News and Features Editor**

"Delightfully zany, melancholy and inventive."
**-Hello!: Thomas Whitaker, Editor**

"Fluent, pictorial, winsome, allegorical - with just the right dollop of quirk!"
**-Andrew Bullock, Daily Mail**

# THE CUCKOO OF AWARENESS

## ANDREW BRUSH

*atmosphere press*

*for Sophie & Noah*

# CONTENTS

Prologue     3

## Part One

Audrey Hepburn     7
Black Swans     8
Symphony Number One in Fucked-Up Major     10
The Festival of Seconds     12
Yippee for Mrs Whippy     15
The Cuckoo of Awareness (I)     20

## Part Two

Krakatoa     31
Wongo the Wonder Dog (I)     39
Wellington Square Garden     41
Man of Gloom     43
Injury Crisis     45
Doughnuts     47
Dusky Thrush     55
Appalachia     58
Barry 'the Birdman' Jones     61
Peter, Paul & Mary     65
The Cuckoo of Awareness (II)     69
Moom Monsters (I)     73
Lafonia     77
Wongo the Wonder Dog (II)     82
Operation Columbo     84

John Denver 88

Sitting Bull 93

W.S.R.C. 97

Moom Monsters (II) 103

Visitation 108

Scarlet Lightning 113

Basilica 115

The Machine of Happiness (I) 117

The Caretaker 118

Jesus 126

Burning Rhyme 131

Whaddney the Robin (I) 134

Burning Rhyme (a dramaticule) 136

National Give Up Pornography Day 142

Moom Monsters (III) 143

Half-time Team Talk 146

Shambles 152

Portrait of Dave 155

Mr Wind 162

T-Minus 13 Verses 164

The Strawberry River 168

Flash Gordon 169

The Cuckoo of Awareness (III) 172

## Part Three

Fridge 177

Hall of Famer 178

Moom Monsters (IV) 181

I Love Wheelbarrow 186

Public Service Announcement 190

A Walk on the Wild Side 192

| | |
|---|---|
| The Secrets of the Rainforest | 196 |
| Big Bird | 197 |
| Dusky Bites the Dust | 199 |
| Farewell Mr Wongo | 201 |
| Moom Monsters (V) | 203 |
| Weaponisation | 207 |
| Body Bags | 209 |
| Casualties | 210 |
| Wongo the Wonder Dog (III) | 212 |
| The Sound of Music | 213 |
| Whaddney the Robin (II) | 215 |
| Gardeners' World | 217 |
| 100% Tolerance | 220 |
| Bubbles | 222 |
| G-Day | 224 |
| Emergency Services | 227 |
| Bad Day at Wellington Square | 228 |
| Time of Death | 231 |
| Pervert's Paradise | 235 |
| Avalon | 239 |
| The Machine of Happiness (II) | 245 |
| Crows | 246 |
| Moving | 247 |
| Moom Monsters (VI) | 251 |

# PROLOGUE

**INFORMATION**
Any thought that I have right now
Isn't worth a shit because I'm totally
Fucked up.
*Richard Brautigan*

He's going to tell you—somewhat poetically—because that's how the 'Cuckoo of Awareness' liked to roll—he's going to start by telling you the tragic story of how the 'fucked-upness' came my way.

'The Cuckoo of Awareness?' Believe me with unwavering certainty he existed, conversed with me, became my cherished friend.

I miss him.

If some folks' grandiose creative delusions stretch to them being Napoleon or Joan of Arc, then please indulge me compassionately with my supernatural Cuckoo of Awareness.

In reality you don't get to choose your brand of madness, it chooses you.

I owe a lot to madness—it saved my life.

History and fate choose you too.

For at the same time as my travails, and by bent of perverse coincidence, my hometown & place of residence became the epicentre of an epoch-making event—'The Battle of Wellington Square'—the most uplifting peacetime civilian massacre in history.

What caused this great event? Triggered it?

The Cuckoo of Awareness will show you.

You could say this is a unique front row, Cuckoo's eyewitness view of both my recuperation and the extraordinary, seemingly random origins of the battle and the lives behind the leading and not so leading protagonists.

As Josephus was the great seminal historian present at the bloodthirsty Siege of Jerusalem, so too the Cuckoo of Awareness was the omnipresent chronicler of the great Battle of Wellington Square—a far more horrifying spectacle.

I am sure, sure as any recovering mad man in remission can be, that the storytelling of these historical and personal events was the medicine he gave me, spoon fed me line by beautiful curing line. What could be more beautiful for you than a cure to read? If you've ever been cured of anything you will know exactly what I mean. I put these vignettes to my lips and drank, poured in by my friend the Cuckoo of Awareness and poured out by the pen of me, Tommy Atkins.

# PART ONE

# AUDREY HEPBURN

This should help put things in perspective. Give you an idea of the enormity of the healing task that lay ahead of me.

There was a white cherry blossom tree in the communal Garden of Wellington Square that flowered (still does) in the second week of March—just in time to catch the eyes of the Cheltenhamshire Festival race-goers. She was so film star beautiful you just couldn't keep your staring camera eyes off her complexion. Sunlight queued up to touch her blossomed face. You wanted to walk out with that tree swinging on your arm. It was a smoking-hot tree, make no mistake.

Each spring, Tom would say cheerfully to his wife, "Audrey Hepburn looks ravishing today." That's how pretty the tree was. It was like the soul of Audrey Hepburn lived in that tree and nourished its white beauty.

That spring, no matter how hard Audrey tried to catch her former admirer's attention, Tom didn't notice her flirtatious advances. Audrey began to think she was losing her touch. When a man doesn't recognise Audrey Hepburn, you know he's got a big pile of troubles on his mind.

I told you it was bad.

# BLACK SWANS

There was a gathering of Black Swans.

The crows could see them, for only the crows and a Cuckoo of Awareness can see such things.

They shuddered under the shadow of their wings.

It's not a good omen when a crow shudders.

If you see a crow shuddering—run like the wind.

The crows had buggered off. Evacuated Wellington Square faster than their crow wings could carry them. The crow population of 'Welly' was now crow-less. They didn't want to be around when the unimaginable magnitude of the brewing thunderstorm struck.

Smart creatures crows.

Trouble was coming to Cheltenhamshire.

One by one, Black Swans carrying with them their rare and unpredictable future events would coalesce into elegant Wellington Square.

A mysterious air-traffic controller who controls the fate of the world had been clearing them for landing: just as he did for the Black Death, for the rise of Adolf Hitler, the sinking of the Titanic, Chernobyl, 9/11, the fall of Lehman Brothers, COVID-19, and now for the impending 'Battle of Wellington Square'.

Very soon events would unfurl. The fiendish flight controller would rub his hands together with excitement before giving the command for the Black Swans to fall in for their fateful mission.

They would link their wings together, parade shuffling

into position. Inspected and cleared for take-off they would fly fate straight to the pre-destined hearts of the unsuspecting. The destiny of Black Swans is always a great drama. A few will always escape the shotgun of history, on the run permanently from zealous historians. The wise after the event will say they 'told us so' and how 'inevitable it all was.'

# SYMPHONY NUMBER ONE IN FUCKED-UP MAJOR

"Days should not have anniversaries," Tom said to himself with a sigh that made the barometer weep, while prematurely ripping June from the BBC Countryfile Calendar. 'Lone Stoat' June lay in crumpled desecrated death, innocent calendar collateral damage. The other months cowered behind May. *If only I could kidnap you, freeze time,* he thought. There is no law against such thoughts. As he was contemplating going on the run with May the crumple of June's body twitched involuntarily—he trod on it, twisting his foot like it was a cigarette butt to silence it.

June—the month that stored the worst day of their lives, of any lives, the dreadful moment, the pain, the source of his sigh within its numeric borders was fast approaching. Unable to think about anything else, the future was rushing towards him at such speed the present was dying before it was born, melting like black snow made of stale time. It would make the saddest snowman you've ever seen. The black day itself wasn't worried; it was blissfully unaware of its own arrival, its own sadness. For some people it would mark the happiest or luckiest day of their lives. It didn't for Tom & Amelia.

When your every waking and barely sleeping thought cannot escape the dreadful heaviness of its own dark gravity it will eventually decide to get its psychotic act together and form a monstrous character, put its smelly feet up and make itself at home rent-free. With a constant supply of highly nutritious savoury snacks and nourishment from the suffer-fest buffet bar of grief, this host was living proof that you are what you eat and think.

Captain Lunatic—a highly decorated present-killer-class U-boat captain—was at the disservice of Thomas (Tommy) Atkins, the irony of which was not lost on the Captain. With peeping periscope pleasure he voyeuristically watched the hull of Tom's mind breaking and tearing like a torpedoed sinking steel ship. "Ja! Ja! Ja! Tommie!" he grunted, whilst jerking-off at the spectacle, feasting on the marrowbone of that stale black snow as if it was his last schnitzel. He couldn't get enough of the black stuff. Lunatic would dig the sweet musical melody of breakdown like he was conducting Beethoven. You wouldn't want to let Lunatic's 'Symphony Number One in Fucked-Up Major' anywhere near your ears.

There they were: Lunatic—bearded, bonkers and woolly-jumpered, looking like Ernest Hemingway on a very bad day—and Tom—somewhere inside his cranium-domed shittiest creek of caged darkness without a paddle.

There wasn't room for both of them; something had to give. It would be a loser-leave-town contest.

# THE FESTIVAL OF SECONDS

It was something instinctive, primordial as migration, that finally broke Tom's May fever; beckoned him, as it had done for most of his life. Like an inspired general in the face of overwhelming odds, he had conceived a plan that would give him a fighting chance of coping with his broken-heartedness. He would choose the terrain and enlist his allies. Akin to Napoleon dressed in waders, he set off courageously from Wellington Square for the Windrush River on a May morning humming with renewal. Something told him there was medicine there and he needed it badly.

Still as a crane, alone beside an adagio river, not a periscope in sight, he watched the Windrush wind blow gently through the poplar colonnade, a silver glittering glissando of leaves belly-up can-canning to rippling applause. A pair of hobbies swooped on the mating mayfly in the canopy while the meditative ancient sound of the trout rising created concentric circles with the divine power to hold time back and pull him into its magnetic attraction. Excitedly, he opened the fly box candy store, still with a sense of wonderment, a ceremony of hope and expectation, a simple joy returning. A grey wulff mayfly was chosen and tied in a half blood knot, moistened with his tongue, tightened and trimmed before its hair was dressed with floatant in a spiky punk rock style.

In the beautiful now, the line tightened with thrashing life cast after cast. He admired each freckled bar as if it were a masterpiece of pointillism before releasing them to their crystal clear gin palace. Absorbed, he had become like the silence of unthinking things, he was moving in the day, breathing with it, his body was returning to life.

Lunatic was dying. Depth charges of fresh time fell on him, dissolving his figment form, leaving the present moment intact. Tom Atkins was being brought back to life.

It takes light eight minutes and twenty seconds to reach the Earth from the sun travelling at a speed of 186,000 miles per second. It doesn't smile with maternal pride when it enters Earth's atmosphere, or have a hope particle. Moonlight is just the reflection of light from the sun—it is not made of romance. Wind is just air moving. Music—vibrations travelling through that air. Clouds are not lonely. Lunatic's only hope of survival now was the arrival of the reality rescue cavalry blowing fearful bugles to scare away Tom's newfound peace of mind.

It was in the ambient light that exposed the previously unseen, when the day held its fragrant breath, clutching time and light to stay and the barn owl circled the field; It was in this stillness amongst the festival of seconds the bugle cruelly sounded and consolation began to die. It was Tom's innocent, happy thought—*it doesn't get any better than this*—that changed the destiny of the day and his life. Frozen, his mind awaited nature's orders but they never came. For he knew that in just a few days the satiated brownies would sink without trace; you would need a black box to detect them. He knew the river would stare back at him with lifeless eyes as if now was only a dream. He knew that when he walked back through the door of his home it would not be the perfect day. He knew that if all the beauty of all the days assembled wherever he went, it would still not be enough. Not by half.

Such thoughts were like reviving schnitzel smelling salts to Lunatic. He unzipped his fly with anticipation. Bonaparte, dejected, retreated from the battlefield.

In the distance, pylons moved across the fields like sturdy farm-worker women hitching their cabled skirts. His rod, like a divining stick, carried him closer and closer. *What if I could make the perfect cast?* he thought, stripping line from his reel and dowsing it in a nearby cattle trough like a thirsty snake. A warm wave of happiness filled Tommy's body.

False casting, he savoured the beauty of the D loop in the champagne light and the comforting growing rocking motion of his body. The smooth, worn cork handle had watched his hands grow older, and each eye guide was a threaded cherished moment in his life. Effortlessly he shot the leader, unfurling into the loving firmament, lassoing the metallic woman; and from the whip-crack of electric light he pulled his smiling son from the day and held him again, smelt him again, was a father again, and didn't let go until he fell into an armless earth humming with renewal.

# YIPPEE FOR MRS WHIPPY

June, despite all Tom's best efforts, arrived, and in doing so created a botched suicide anniversary waiting eagerly to be added to next year's Countryfile calendar. Dispersed into a shattered brokenness, Lunatic accompanied him to the krankenhausen. Invisible to Tom, only others could see his un-mendable looking stare. Tom's hands now trembled almost enough to crack his whole fragile body unless held. He had reached the zenith, the peak of fucked-up mountain.

Tommy and Lunatic swallowed the antipsychotic medication and together floated in them like two zombies in a lifeboat through many helpless months before they finally washed back up on a beach called home.

'Yippee! It's Mr Whippy!' That's what it said on the vintage 1960s Commer Karrier BF ice cream van resplendent in its original cream and pink livery. Two giant cones similar to Olympic torches decorated the front of the van like vertical eyebrows. To the left of the serving counter the original menu paraded the ice creams for sale: Cones (with a base that looked like a large paint brush), Golden Vanilla Choc Ice, Dark and Golden Choc Ice, Orange Fruitie and Pineapple & Strawberry Split, Woppa, Funny Faces and Sky Ray...Classic '99' with flake.

It arrived silently at midnight like the Mary Celeste on wheels, its 'greensleeves' chime kept up its green sleeves for another time. It was actually Mrs Whippy, not Mr

Whippy, that helped sow the seeds that put his life back on the right track during the month of No Hope November.

He would always wonder at where the mobile volunteer social worker came from? Who she was? Perhaps she had read the obituaries months before in the local paper or been present at the hospital? The funeral? Somewhere right now was parked that ice cream van of mercy—in the equivalent of the bat cave or garage, or maybe it was outside the house of some other poor bastard in need of help? He'd never seen the van or the mysterious driver before or since. She would never know how much he wanted to thank her, how grateful he would always be to her. It was like a restless fragment of gratitude that would always be unfulfilled until it docked with her eyes once more and could be put to rest. There is a fragile chain of human atoms like Mrs Whippy that peel the earth with compassion with everyday acts of unpaid human kindness. They are very special atoms. They wipe the dribble from smiling human mouths, they hold hands, they listen on the end of a phone, they lift & push; they offer an arm for support, they volunteer selflessly, they check on, they deliver meals, they don't walk past, they see and they find you. They find You. They are all blackbirds singing the song of the soul.

It was midnight, the exact time it said on the lovingly handmade written card anonymously posted to him:

*Dear Mr Atkins,*

*Please accept this invitation to meet with me tomorrow outside your home at midnight. I do hope you will join me.*

It didn't seem in the least bit threatening. Granted it was bloody weird. Why not? He was curious and he didn't sleep much anyway these days; the nighttime had just become a place where the loom of his mind just spun more gloomy darkness out of darkness.

Tom stood on the porch steps turning up his coat collar against the crisp cold coming from a November sky, bathed by the light of Cygnus and a full moon. Today was coming in clean and perfect.

Across the night sky, clouds rippled like wet sand on a beach making you want to run across it bare footed. *Welcome to Cheltenhamshire On Sea* thought Tom. As he walked the short steps along the front path to the gate, the song of his clicking shoes in the still night air pulled him up. It was an echo that once had a stepping out cheerfulness but now it bounced back like a haymaker of longing, reminding him of how far he had moved away from life's simple pleasures. In that brief moment, the thought of the sound of a large family holiday tent zip unzipping into a new day smelling full of promise and hope came to him. It made him sad. His mind was very creative when it came to making him sad.

As he approached the van, he began to read the menu. A woman in her early 60s appeared at the counter. She was wearing a plus size coatigan in lilac with turned-up cuffs. Her plump curvaceous body and appearance looked like it had been poured from the Mr Whippy tap by the hand of the artist Beryl Cook.

"Mrs Whippy, I presume," he said before continuing, "a Classic '99' with flake please."

Mrs Whippy gave him her best Mrs Whippy red lipstick barmaid smile. She had a lusty, irrepressible air. Her blonde hair had been freshly coloured and coiffured into a bouncy bob still smelling of the salon's hairspray. She wore too much opal eye shadow that inexplicably suited her. The canvas of her skin still held enough elasticity for her make-up to be applied without cracking. This stranger he thought had spent time in the mirror with her own secrets and thoughts of a life of which he knew absolutely nothing about. What he did know was that before closing the door of her home and setting sail for her rendezvous with him she had sprayed herself with a nerve agent perfume that could overpower a small army.

The words, "To what do I owe this pleasure, Midnight Woman," never left his lips—instead they went up in smoke with his dragon's breath that filled the air. As Tom went to speak he was pulled up short by her large hypnotic emerald eyes. It was as if her round face was merely designed as a setting for those precious kind crystals. Her irises were such an inclusion of humanity and serenity that they could only have been burned from knowing something of what he had been through. She knew, he thought. At that moment a door opened. "Come in," she said amiably, "it's cosy in here."

Mrs Whippy had given the van an impressive makeover. "Please sit down," she said, pointing to some lavish, lushly quilted deep-buttoned banquet seating strewn with colourful tasselled Moroccan cushions in different shapes and sizes. It was a miniature mix of gypsy caravan and Sultan's tent. A fold down dressed Formica wooden wall table separated the seating area where she now rested her large ring-less soft hands. Any moment now he was expecting the crystal ball and tarot cards to appear.

If ever a woman had the appearance of a talker it was Mrs Whippy; she looked like she was made up of a lot of life stories, and yet she said nothing.

Mrs Whippy's eyes were like loving bomb bays opened wide. A payload of love fell from their light, blasting the edifice of Tom's coping like the bursting Dambuster walls of the Sorpe dam. Tom let it all out; let it unravel before her silence.

When it was over, when he was spent of so much pain and anger, she helped steady Tom down the steps and led him back to the front gate of his house. Above them the sky tide had come in and covered the beach.

"Go out in search of the Cuckoo," she said squeezing his hand before turning and leaving.

"Why do you think she only wanted to see me?" said Tom, drained with emotion as he crawled into bed.

"I don't know," said Amelia, not in the least bit curious.

Both of them lay in bed on their sides, buckled up tenderly together, each getting ready to separately deep-sea dive—to submerge into their individual worlds of grief and emptiness knowing that when they ascended the sun would rise into another day without their son.

What Amelia didn't say was that she had already met with Mrs Whippy the previous week following exactly the same invitation. That night, Tom's body actually rediscovered some sleep. He fell asleep wondering whether in his emotional state Mrs Whippy really did say the strangest thing: "Go out in search of the Cuckoo"?

# THE CUCKOO OF AWARENESS (I)

I am the Cuckoo of Awareness. I live happily enlightened in the lime tree in the communal garden opposite number 8 Wellington Square, the home of Tom and Amelia Atkins.

Bonfire night was full of acoustic surprises, but none more so than the first cuckoo in November. As Tom stared out deep in troubled thought from the desk of his favourite study window into that pyrotechnic night, I launched my first cuckoo communication firework without the need for a cuckoo whistle; it was au natural:

"Coo-Coo."

"That's a peculiar firework," Tom mused to himself.

"Did you know a Chinese chef invented them? Mixed up the wrong ingredients in his wok—bang! Would like to have seen that on Masterchef!" I replied.

Tom was used to hearing a voice in his head but it still took him by surprise, especially as it was one he hadn't heard before:

"Jesus Christ who the hell are you!?" Tom said, understandably alarmed.

"I am the Cuckoo of Awareness—you're supposed to be looking for me, remember? I'm here to help you, to finish the fine work Mrs Whippy started."

"What do you mean, here to help me? You should have been in Africa months ago. Mrs Whippy never mentioned a Cuckoo with awareness!"

"It's an ancient Tibetan saying Tom, 'Go out in search

of the Cuckoo'—a metaphor for starting the healing process."

"Metaphors aren't supposed to exist!"

"This one is alive and kicking. For the record Tom, I'm not your common or garden Cuckoo but an ancient Tibetan Cuckoo, a direct descendant of the great Buddha himself! People call me Purusa-damya-sarathi or 'tamer of men' due to my great talent in calming fears and agitation. Now—as for that fragrant saint and vigilante of kindness, she can be a bit slapdash on detail."

"The last time I went out in search of something in nature's great realm it ended badly, very badly, and for your record you're not calming my fears!"

"You came so close, Tom."

"Close to what?"

"To killing Lunatic," I said, lowering my voice.

"I don't want to hear his name," replied Tom, unnerved. First meetings with patients can be a bit tricky.

"I can eliminate the Captain, remove him from the nest of your mind."

"Well you should know all about removing things from nests—at least he knew how to build one! He's now been promoted to Rear Admiral following his last successful campaign."

"Last week at the pedestrian crossing he told you to step out in front of a car."

"A red Volkswagen."

"Made in Germany?"

"Yep."

"Who says Germans don't have a sense of humour?"

"He's hilarious."

"You came very close to obeying him, Tom, I heard you

shout No! To the voice in your head, you only just pulled yourself back in time."

"Close."

"Would you like to hear about the time I cured Marcus Aurelius?"

"No."

"He was a pupil of mine; by the time I had finished with him he went from strength to strength—became Roman Emperor and lived every act of his life as if it were his last—that's my boy!"

"Listen Cockoo, I'm tired, I don't want to be a Roman Emperor, I just want to escape from this mind, from you, please do me a favour and fly away—one interlocutor is bad enough let alone two!"

"Let me sing you my cuckoo song, Tom."

"No please don't."

"It will help you escape, it's the source of my enlightenment."

"I've heard it for Christ's sake, it only has two syllables, it's hardly the dawn chorus!"

"Indulge me."

"Let's get this over with then."

Even now after centuries of gigs worldwide I get a little nervous. I cleared my throat and performed my song Dylanesque in the blues style with some harmonica accompaniment thrown in between lines. Here are the simple lyrics and chords in E if you want to join in:

E7
*The nature of multiplicity is nondual*
*and things in themselves are pure and simple;*

A7
*being here and now is thought-free*
*and it shines out in all forms, always all good;*


B7
*it is already perfect, so the striving sickness is avoided*
*and spontaneity is constantly present.*


*(Lyrics taken from the sacred Tibetan text of the Tun-huang manuscript now housed in the British Library and discovered by archaeologist and explorer Sir Aurel Stein at Tun-huang in remote northwest China from the 'Caves of a Thousand Buddhas', a labyrinth of nearly 500 caves and a treasure trove of ancient Buddhist artefacts and one of the least known wonders of the world. The six verses of the Cuckoo's Song of Total Presence introduce the total presence of the nature of mind.)*


"Catchy little number, isn't it?" I said, filling the awkward silence that greeted me at the end of my performance. You don't become the enlightened magical King of Birds without being a great singer-songwriter.

"No, it's not," said Tom bluntly.

"Trust me, it will grow on you."

"I listened, it didn't work, goodbye."

"We haven't started yet!"

"Tell me, Great Tamer of Men, have you been able to help everyone with your terrible cuckoo song?"

"Yes."

"Really?" said Tom, detecting a fraction of hesitation in my voice.

"There was one that was sublimely untameable; he

became a dear friend," I said, unable to disguise an air of sadness.

"Who?"

"It doesn't matter Tom, I'm here for you, mate."

"Who?" Tom insisted.

"There is a thing called patient confidentiality, Tom."

"Let's call it taking up references before I decide whether or not to let you into my mind, but don't go getting your cuckoo hopes up; anyway, my lips are sealed."

"Arthur."

"Arthur who?"

"Arthur Rimbaud—Rimb, a great French poet."

"Yes, yes I know who he is, '"Let it come, let it come, the season we can love,'" said Tom, quoting Rimb with a flourish. "He finished writing nearly all his great works by the age of 18. Being an ex English Literature teacher has its simple showing-off advantages. Imagine having Rimbaud sat in your English class?"

"You will one day, Tom, a female Rimbaud to be factual."

"Please don't patronise me."

"With my help you will return to work, Tom."

"Hahahaaaaa"—Tom laughed with more than just a touch of hysteria; he'd loved his job.

"'Look out, here comes Mr Atkins, he's had a mental breakdown, tried to top himself...'" he said pulling a goofy cross-eyed face. Tom got to his feet as if addressing a class. "'Okay, kids, get your notebooks out, today we're going to look at synonyms for crazy, who wants to kick us off?'

"'Bananas, sir.'

"'A classic, but surely we can come up with some more?'

"'Screw loose, sir.'

"'Or missing Freya, don't forget the missing screw—they disappear from too much rattling.'" Tom mimicked the rattling by shaking his body and making a silly raspberry noise by rubbing his finger over his lips.

"'Loon, sir.'

"'You will like this one Tamer of Men.'

"'Cuckoo, sir.'

"'It's in those oo's, something crazy resides in those circles,'" he said, twirling his index finger anti-clockwise at his temple.

"'Bonkers, sir.'

"'A personal favourite, don't the consonants sound great?'

"'Insane in the membrane, sir.'

"'I'm liking your work soldier, much more imaginative.'

"'Two fries short of a happy meal, sir.'

"'You're on a roll now.'

"'Fucked up, sir.'

"'Go to the top of the class, Johnny, now that's what I'm talking about! Class disss-missed!'"

Animated and a little manic, Tom slumped back down in his chair, his head slightly bowed. I let the silence settle before continuing:

"Clever kid that, Johnny," I said with my dry cuckoo of awareness wit.

"Not as clever as Rimbaud," said Tom regaining his composure. "You were going to tell me about him?"

"Was I?"

"Yes, you are."

"He was a scared boy, Tom, he built his poetry out of

his father's abandonment, we got that far."

"What happened?" said Tom, enthusiastic to hear more.

"He was a wild child, a force of nature, he shined with such a rare light as a pupil, I became very fond of him, loved him like a father."

"You got too close?"

"Yes, for the first and last time in my long life. I may be enlightened but I'm not perfect, Tom, and there are limits to my powers. Like a parent, I asked him to promise me that one day he would return to poetry when the time was right. Would you like to hear a literary world exclusive, Tom?"

"Yes, my ears love them, tell me."

"It's a previously unknown and unpublished poem. Just before he left for his travels he dedicated this last poem to me:

### Pour Coucou
Like a comet
Starlight pouring out of my arse
I will disappear out of sight
Of the gazing world
To gather a new tenderness.


Look! Here comes crazy Rimbaud back again!
A marvel of old as fuckness—a ripened rebel.
I will explode a great love
Fire words warm when read.
Then, into a season not yet known
My initials inscribed in stone.

"Pure Rimbaud," said Tom smiling. "He never returned to poetry, did he?"

"The cancer beat my boy to it. I was there at the end, he was just 37. The season 'not yet known' was late autumn. The comet was returning, Tom, with such lovely sounding words to light up the world again, to explode a great love."

"That would have been some much needed explosion, cuckoo."

"Yes it would have been Tom, far better than the fireworks outside."

"Do you have any other literary world exclusives in your locker?" asked Tom, unable to quell his enthusiasm for the subject.

"Does the name Shakespeare ring any bells?" I said enticingly.

"You're hired!" said Tom.

In celebration of his sudden unexpected announcement a firework exploded colourfully in the sky outside. It was a stem to Tom's past.

"Do you remember when you invented the Moom Monsters stories for Freddie at bedtime and the fireworks exploding over Murria?" I said, mentioning his son for the first time.

Like a warm wind the memory blew inside him—his heart ached in the wind—he remembered his young son endearingly pointing at the Moon with his tiny finger and saying Moom. 'Moom, Daddy! Moom, Mummy!' It became part of their family folklore. When the wind stopped he said, full of pride and a lump of love in his throat:

"He loved them, didn't he?"

"He certainly did, I loved them myself," I said.

"I'm going to bed to try and get your singing out of my head," said Tom.

"You won't regret it," I said.

"I certainly won't, your singing is bloody awful," he said.

Each day we went to work at my cuckoo call, always starting with the 'Cuckoo Song.'

# PART TWO

# KRAKATOA

Without a guide you won't see Black Swans coming—not a chance—they are always cloaked in extreme probability like the brittle rivets on the bow of the Titanic. Let me begin with the first Black Swan rumbles, the rumbles that led to the rumble to end all rumbles!

Every bloodthirsty battle needs a source of anger. In the early part of the 21$^{st}$ century there was no shortage of anger to go around. No one was running out of anger ammunition.

The molten anger boiling inside generations of long suffering Cheltenhamshire council taxpayers would, when it exploded, make Krakatoa's volcanic eruption—equivalent to 200 megatons of TNT—look like a party popper.

At the epicentre of this rage was the proud magnum opus of the local Highways & Parking Department—the envy of the uncivilised world—Cheltenhamshire's one and only one-way system. It truly deserved status as the 8$^{th}$ Wonder of the World. It was an absolute beauty.

To call it simply a one-way system would be an insult to its magnificence. It was a gravitational time machine harvesting the precious hours of innocent townsmen and townswomen's lives, a living monument to motoring and pedestrian misery, a circular torture chamber. It was a prison full of inmates rattling its bars hysterically: "Let me out! Let me out! I'm innocent!"

The locals had even coined their own name for it—

Guantanamo, named after the notorious detention camp. Like its inmates, you never knew when you were going to be allowed to leave, often detained indefinitely without trial.

The police and emergency services were well prepared for the inevitable outburst of fury and civil unrest that would ensue once Krakatoa erupted—they'd assigned a special code name to deal with such an event: Operation Krakatoa. They regularly rehearsed coordinated practice simulations for its eventuality. There had been a few recent false alarms for the police volcanologists. Some early warning signs of volcanic activity appeared when thousands of demonstrators wearing orange prisoner uniforms linked arms and laid down in Guantanamo chanting anti one-way system songs of revolution; immediately after stuffing one final double chocolate chip muffin into her mouth, one brave young woman who described herself as carrying 'a few extra pounds' declared she was going on hunger strike, whilst another young man nailed his scrotum to the tarmac. It was not surprising when you consider that Guantanamo was firmly on Amnesty International's radar due to its major breaches of human rights.

Within the Cheltenhamshire Chancellery offices, Supreme Commander Aloysius Gittler led the council's crack Highways & Parking Team. The personal details of the senior leaders remained a closely guarded secret to protect them from acts of justified violence. The team used the latest super computers to proudly fine-tune Guantanamo to inflict the maximum amount of inconvenience and delays on its public. It also used the more traditional methods at its disposal, such as commencing roadworks during racing, science, and literary and jazz festivals. A tweak to the bus timetables here, a new pedestrian and kamikaze zebra crossing there. No self-respecting zebra that valued their life would set a hoof on one, strategically positioned as they were to bring pedestrians and motorists into maximum accident conflict.

Passenger-less post apocalypse buses with zombie drivers at the helm and no route number or destination, circumnavigated the 8$^{th}$ Wonder of the World perpetually as if cursed to eternal punishment by a Greek God. The buses arrived every 5 minutes. The speechless 'Out of Service' drivers and will-less servants of the Highways & Parking Team stopped at all Guantanamo's bus stops. Inside, the buses were brand spanking new with plastic still covering the unused seats. The commuters stared at the empty buses, the zombie's stared straight ahead, drivers stared at the backs of the empty buses—stark staring raving mad it was. For all intents and purposes the buses had become mobile congestion and advertising machines.

### (Bus Lanes)

I've outcast these two words on the page as a mark of protest and solidarity with Cheltshireons—quarantined them with steel brackets.

The bus lanes' effectiveness in creating misery for Cheltenhamshire's commuters was unparalleled. It quickly became the preferred fashionable weapon of choice for Gittler and his highways henchman. It was a legal weapon of awesome power that they could fire at will. Gittler and his team licked their lips with excitement at any new prospect of unleashing its unspeakable congestion capabilities; commuters licked their lips at any prospect of travelling on it. Where once there was the practicality of two 'brothers in arms' lanes working in collaboration to aid rush hour circulation, now there was just single road bottlenecks of tailback beauty. Without warning, often in the dead of night, brothers and sisters across the town had been cruelly separated from each other, amputated to live less rewarding and meaningful lives as bus lanes.

Gittler commissioned flags for the staff cars of the High Command so that they could travel on the bus lanes like royalty.

The High Command carefully monitored the prisoners by C.C.T.V., ensuring traffic flow was minimised at all times. Gittler had a vast network of willing accomplices on his secret payroll. The bin men and women were in on the act, collecting refuse during the morning and afternoon commute with maximum road hogging inconsideration. Wino's and the homeless hung out at pedestrian crossings, just pressing the button all day long—easy money. Zebra crossings became Zimmer crossings to help supplement disability benefits. Council lorries would break down and shed loads inexplicably in the worst possible places.

Appointments were missed, children were late for or stranded at school, commerce ground to a standstill, delivery goods perished, pollution filled the lungs, asthma attacks attacked with more ferocity, and quality family time was diminished. The school holidays were normally a time that brought a degree of welcome peace and respite to the roads. Not in Gittlershire. Gittler replaced the school run with a 'special measures' mobile operations taskforce to choke the flow of traffic to pre holiday levels. It was costly but worth every penny.

Everything had proceeded perfectly to Gittler's grand fundamentalist plan. Centuries from now, some historians would argue that Gittler was a visionary, a radical long-term thinker who bravely refused to fall victim to the gratification of short-termism and populism. They would strongly contest he was a man way ahead of his time, a man trying to end our obsession with the motorcar by making the driving experience such a hell on this earth that people would be forced to give up their vehicles for the greater good of humanity. They would also deny that he had caused misery and suffering to thousands.

The historians were talking bollocks. Gittler had a Napoleonic Complex. He was suffering from undiagnosed Short Man Syndrome. In the middle of the 21$^{st}$ century scientists would discover the gene carrying this illness, offering hope of a cure to millions. At just 5 feet, 3 inches Gittler wasn't well, and neither were his senior officers, none of whom looked down on him. That's why they were raging war on the public: it was in their genes.

Gittler generated so much income for the council that they turned a blind eye—he was untouchable. Gittler was the 'Ernst Stavro Blofeld' of congestion masterminds, with an international underworld network to his Short Man & Woman Syndrome brothers and sisters. The flag of North Korea recently flew proudly over the Chancellery offices, welcoming a delegation from their great leader.

Each morning at 07.30am sharp before sending them into battle, Field Marshall Gittler would take the salute as he paraded his elite regiment of traffic warden soldiers with all the marching precision of the cold stream guards. The basic training to join the regiment was renowned for its toughness—only ten percent of applicants made it into public service. Gittler's team had no weaknesses; they had no heartstrings to pull on. They were a callous and cold-blooded bunch of hand picked critters. There was no point appealing to their better nature—they didn't have one. What's more, they were fast: they could write a penalty notice ticket in five seconds flat. Less than that—pack your bags—you're on your way home.

Nationwide, most traffic wardens wear blue uniforms that are too big for them, giving them a slightly comical Dopey look from the seven dwarfs. There would be no place for them in Gittler's army. They wore all black uniforms tailor made by Hugo Boss: double breasted tunic jackets with two hip pockets, white shirts and black ties with 'Civil Enforcement Officer' insignia on their epaulets, collars and black caps. Belt buckles were inscribed with a picture of a car crushed in a giant fist. Black tricot trousers were worn tucked into their calf-high black jackboots. Greatcoats were issued for inclement weather.

Many of his team had been highly decorated; they proudly wore their distinguished ticketing red and black armbands for outstanding action in the field. The greater the number of red stripes the higher the decoration. Gittler's hypnotic steel blue eyes along with his leadership and powerful oratory had convinced them that they were the finest Cheltenhamshire had to offer. He bewitched them and commanded their complete loyalty and dedication. Day in, night out they completed their missions, prepared to die for Gittler and his just cause.

Gittler and senior members of the council had recently

been gifted shares in the asset management company that owned the town centre multi-storey car park and retail units in exchange for some 'improvements' to traffic access. This was a win-win situation. It provided Gittler a welcome boost towards his retirement pension as well as enabling him to implement the final solution of his plan.

The improvements marked the last brush stroke, the final tap of the chisel to the masterpiece. The only remaining sane and effective section of the one-way system had fallen, making access to the north of Cheltenhamshire impossible. The entire team stood back proudly from their crowning glory like they were Michelangelo or Leonardo da Vinci, admiring their artistic endeavours.

"I hereby declare this monstrous fuck up well and truly open."

That's not what Gittler said with proud tears rolling down his eyes when he cut the red tape on the new section of Guantanamo opposite the Town Hall—but that was closest to the truth.

A larger number of people than expected turned up to witness the opening ceremony, staring out with dead eyes from the windows of their motionless vehicles. This was the icing on the Guantanamo cake and just made the occasion all the more special for Gittler and his team. Many of the victims were clutching their steering wheels, sobbing uncontrollably; one woman's heart just gave up the will to beat any further, whilst another just went mad screaming hysterically—her mental breakdown was most inconsiderate as it just triggered a chain reaction of other people losing their minds. Car horns rang out with the sound of madness. One man, having considered carefully all the beautiful life options available to him, correctly concluded it was best just to set fire to himself.

There was only so much pain these people could take.

# WONGO THE WONDER DOG (I)

AWOOooo!—That seems as good a way as any to introduce a particular favourite of mine—'Wongo the Wonder Dog.' Wongo, unlike other dogs living in Wellington Square, didn't actually howl, or religiously practice howling as if he were in training for the howling world championships.

There was a classy Afghan dame called Bubbles who lived in the Eastern approaches that howled for Britain—her owner, like at least five percent of the British population, was a zoophile. Residents thought the dog was howling because she'd joined the dog choir and was just doing what the hound breed does best. She wasn't—she was howling because her owner was fucking her. The howling was slightly different to the everyday variety—it was a consensual howl of pleasure. Her owner loved her. Every day he told Bubbles he loved her. He knew the average life span of his lover was just 13 years; it would break his heart when she died. The future would soon put an end to this unnecessary heartbreak. Robot dogs and other animatronic creatures designed for the different zoophile community tastes would replace Bubbles. With regular maintenance and software updates they would outlive their partners. Any good-old-days nostalgic desires animals like Bubbles may have harboured to fall in love with humans and have intercourse with them in the future would be gone forever, replaced by robots in a brave new world.

Wongo was a cross between a Bedlington terrier and a whippet. He didn't smell too bad, moult his hair or beg for food, he didn't have a bad bone in his scruffy body and only carried one or two fleas on him at any one time. If you were ever down on your luck he would have made a great begging dog because Wongo was just so cute.

Wongo was permanently moronically happy. He was not the brightest creature on four legs. His owners shelled out a lot of money for a professional dog trainer to try and teach him basic commands. Wongo ignored him and just Wongo'd around in the land of Wongolia. The pro dog trainer thought Wongo was as deaf as a haddock, so he sent Wongo off to the vets for a hearing test that he proceeded to pass with flying bat-like colours. His owner thought that this made Wongo a genius—it didn't.

Next up was the electronic dog collar therapy. The high voltage encouragement just made Wongo happier— he liked nothing more than electricity coursing through his body, preferring it far more to the tasty beef and rabbit dog treat bribes. Wongo would take electrons over beef and rabbit snacks any day. Defeated, the dog trainer gave up. Instead of finding its way onto eBay, Wongo's owners found a good home for that collar—the second drawer down of their bedside table; it quickly became a firm favourite and welcome addition to the kinky repertoire of their healthy sexual experimentation.

Wongo's male owner was an unknown poet; he got a lot of inspiration from his long daily dog walks with Wongo. Despite this, he'd never managed to give Wongo the recognition he deserved and write him into one of his poems after a lifetime on the sidelines.

# WELLINGTON SQUARE GARDEN

Let's get our bearings. It was the spaciousness of my home, the communal Garden of Wellington Square, that gave it an air of leisure and tranquillity. It could accommodate one and a half generous football pitches. Instead of advertising hoardings it had boxed hedges about the height of Aintree racecourses Becher's Brook. Perfect for homing hedgehogs and losing cricket balls in. Sadly there were considerably more cricket balls hogging the hedge than our dear friends the hedgehogs these days.

Four green architectural wrought iron Victorian gates were centrally positioned at the four points of the evergreen hedge compass. Each entrance led to an oval path that circumnavigated the garden, providing an excellent racetrack for young children learning to cycle. When they'd mastered that, the garden gave them ample trees of varying difficulty to climb, swing in and fall out of. Small treasure tree and shrub islands decorated the garden like green atolls with the green sea gently lapping at their shores.

Three mature holm oaks provided the perfect evergreen all-year-round canopy for the homeless to sleep rough under and in so doing delivered a cost effective, sustainable, and permanent solution to Cheltenhamshire's homeless problem. The council were busy all over the town planting holm oaks for future generations of homeless to enjoy.

When the children had finished observing the sleeping

habits of the homeless they could then introduce themselves to the needles and detritus the everyday drug addicts thoughtfully left behind. If ever Britain's rarest mammals—the Wombles of Wimbledon Common—were the subject of short-sighted public sector cutbacks, there was a job waiting for them right here in 'Welly,' providing they wore protective gloves. The last thing we want is the bad publicity of multiple tetanus Womble deaths on our hands. A joyous uplifting civilian massacre on our soil we welcome with open arms, but the rotting corpse of Uncle Bulgaria we do not. The defection of the Wombles to Wellington Square (the Wombles of Wellington Square) would certainly be a huge publicity coup requiring very little rebranding. The residents could wake each morning to their Welly Wombling song as they went about their work.

Outside of the garden a generous grass verge was home to further specimen trees whose lovely poetry had been lost to the local residents due to the fact that they now merely represented a bomber command home for pigeon squadron to shit on their parked cars.

# MAN OF GLOOM

The Man of Gloom was scared of dying. Shit scared. He thought about dying every day of his gloomy life. He would probably think about dying when he was dead. He was also scared of the dark and figured there was going to be a lot of darkness when he died, which scared him even more.

If you're scared of dying you might want to move on to the next chapter.

This chapter is not going to cheer you up.

You are not going to bookmark this page to return to in your darkest hour of need when you need hope.

Today, like every day, he had been having deathly thoughts. He'd been worrying about what might be the cause of his death? The time? The month? The place? What would it be like fighting and arm wrestling with it? How could the body be defeated by the desperate wishes of the mind to live? What would be the last thing he said or looked at? Heard? How many people would turn up at the funeral? His fear spread from himself, to his loved ones—he can't bear to think of them being dead either after he's dead. How can something as beautiful as love die?

These grim mortal contemplations led to the fear being upon the Man of Gloom. Fear fell in his mind like an elevator without gravity. He descended into a terrible tailspin of dread, unable to pull himself up. The ejector seat handle failed repeatedly; in fact it came off in his hand. Saliva stalled inside his mouth and all bodily instruments malfunctioned.

He was going to die and nothing could stop it. The black box was recording: "Oh God, I'm going to die!"

He was travelling at the speed of fear; at that velocity you cannot grab anything to stop your descent; he became a terrornaut.

Terrified, the Man of Gloom ran from his flat in the Southern approaches, running with death at his heels into the Garden Square. He was seeking refuge from his mortality. He was the gingerbread man running as fast as he can and death was the fox. He only had fear to fight the fear of death with and he knew nobody had ever turned away death with fear.

Against all odds—for defeating the fear of death was not easy—against all odds, a benevolent unseen superhero applied the brakes; grabbed hold of the bolting reins, pulling him up slowly, decompressing the bends of dread from his body.

The superhero life-saviour left before the Man of Gloom had time to thank him. The scared-of-dying panic attack had come to an end. If you're going to have a panic attack then the thought of senseless oblivion is most worthy of panicking. If this doesn't make you panic nothing will. The near death experience had heightened his senses. He sat on the solitary garden bench happy to be alive. The fear had been replaced with an almost religious joy of living as the sun warmed his smiling face. Out of this great panic something good would rise, he thought to himself. Then it came to him in a flash of gloomy inspiration. The Man of Gloom conceived the Scared of Dying Society (S.O.D.S.), a self-help group to support terrornauts everywhere.

# INJURY CRISIS

The list of strikers' injuries at Cheltenhamshire Town FC in nearby Whaddon Road read like this:

Hamstring
Severe Infection (waxing legs)
Groin/Pelvis (night out)
Chronic Bowel Condition
Dislocated Jaw (sustained while shouting at referee).

Stretching back to last season the Robins hadn't scored a goal in 11 consecutive matches, equalling the football league's record. The caretaker manager had been forced to recall Perry Mummford (The Mummy), a solid journeyman centre forward who could usually be relied upon to score 10–15 goals a season, but who, like a golfer who had contracted the 'yips' with his putter or a dart player that had 'dartitis' and could not release the arrows, Perry Mummford couldn't score in front of goal or at any angle to goal for that matter. The local press described his catastrophic loss of form and confidence as 'The Curse of the Mummy'. The club only renewed his contract because the fans adored him for his 'walking like an Egyptian' goal celebration made all the more hysterical by his skinny tall frame, knobbly knees and rolled-down socks, all accompanied by the fans singing in celebration the classic 80s Bangles hit, which was said to be responsible for a large part of pre-season ticket sales. The Mummy was to wear the number 7 jersey on Saturday afternoon, which the new gaffer eruditely pointed out was considered by ancient Egyptians to be a symbol of perfection and effectiveness, something that had been in somewhat short supply.

# DOUGHNUTS

In a basement garden flat sandwiched within the Cotswold stone-buttered gothic revival terrace of the Western approaches, just a few doors down from the Atkins, a mysterious ultra-secret cell calling themselves the 'Doughnuts' met.

The Doughnuts minded their own business so artfully that the last thing you would do is actually notice them. They were unnoticeable. They did not care for the ceremonial garments and elaborate trappings of many secret societies: no masonic handshakes, no Grand Master or Knight of the Doughnut, no fraternal blood declarations, no white pointy hats and robes, not even the sporting of horned animal headgear. The Doughnuts were part pranksters and part ethical vigilante spies of fortune, organised for the amusement of themselves and the benefit of others.

They operated undetected just beyond the shadowy shadow of Government Communications Headquarters (GCHQ), the UK's secretive eavesdropping centre known locally as 'The Doughnut.' This was not surprising, as come Monday morning they would all be back at work in the jammy saturated fat heart of that doughnut.

While doughnuts tend to retain their delicious contents, a more appropriate architectural design for GCHQ (excluding the more obvious and frankly imaginative pair of giant ears) would have been a colander; the place leaked like a sieve straight into the ears of the local residents.

Despite the squiggling of their signatures over the Official Secrets Act and some sophisticated interrogation conditioning (for all intents and purposes a modern take on 'name, rank and serial number'), employees of GCHQ were, through absolutely no fault of their own, easily compromised.

For over 60 years GCHQ had been Cheltenhamshire's largest employer; everybody knew somebody who worked there or had a family member on the payroll. Therein lay the problem.

Cheltshireons had over six decades of interrogation practice, or 'quizzing' as it preferred to be respectfully known as in these parts. Quizzing had been handed down from generation to generation like a meme; it had eclipsed cheese rolling and skittles as the most popular local cultural traditions. Quizzing is best described as a kind of skilful parlour game played all year round. The game began with the quizzer asking the perfectly harmless boilerplate question: "What do you do for a living?" Most competent quizzers already knew the answer, given that all GCHQ workers had very large heads and displayed a clumsy awkwardness in social situations. Like so many geniuses, they were on a unique behavioural spectrum, which was integral to them being recruited in the first place—the defence of the nation depends heavily on an unequal opportunities policy.

"I work at GCHQ." Game on.

In the less-experienced quizzer's hands the game was over very quickly: there was a well-rehearsed soft-shoe conversational shuffle in which the 'contestant' could reliably call upon his or her expensive conditioning training to body swerve imprisonment and betraying their beloved country. However, for a master player of the game, known as a 'wormer' (because they could worm anything out of people), the contestant had very little hope of winning. A wormer (remember to add two r's when pronouncing this word for the authentic local dialect) could expertly pick the locks of the contestant's mental training, turning their cerebral dials like a safe cracker, and before they knew it a highly classified mother lode of the world's greatest secrets was gushing forth. It was rare these days that a veteran wormer heard secrets they had not heard countless times before from other contestants, but this is why they did it: for the sheer unbridled joy of a rare new revelation. The very same reason golfers return to the golf course or metal detectorists to the field: that glorious hope of a lower score, a hole in one, a Saxon gold hoard.

Quizzing in Cheltenhamshire even had its own members club with a waiting list to join longer than the M.C.C. The Q Club had its headquarters at Cobblers Corner: a legendary establishment for the repairing of shoes, the cutting of keys and the latest news and gossip from GCHQ. If you wanted to know what was going on in this town, or any other town for that matter, then all you had to do was stick your long nose into Cobblers Corner and seek out the affable proprietary elves Tap and Stitch, the undisputed worming champions and keepers of the worming archives. Each Friday after work, the Q Club met at the Snoop pub where wormers loved to hold court at the bar and catch up on the week's latest matches, and reminisces in time-honoured sporting tradition.

Given the fact that this information was now firmly in

the public domain, I see no reason not to share some of the juiciest fruits of the wormer's craft combined with a little eavesdropping of our own; after all, what's good for the GCHQ goose is good for the gander...

Britain did not have a net debt of 140 billion; there was a giant surplus, not a deficit; in fact, Britain was the wealthiest country on the planet. The only fly in the fiscal ointment was that Her Majesty's Treasury Department hadn't worked out how to cook the books without raising a few eyebrows! GCHQ had gone rogue. It was now nothing more than a gigantic casino that made Caesar's Palace look like a bingo hall. The talented civil servants had become addicted gamblers—yes, there were a few noble men and women who found time for terrorism and cyber-crime, but they were a fading bunch.

The 'eyes in the sky' were now the ultimate high rollers. The house rules ensured the dice were always stacked in their eaves dropping favour. Within the sugar-encrusted walls of the building, winning cheers and celebrations constantly filled the air like the Moulin Rouge as winning bets and trades were landed. It was not surprising they had not detected under their very noses the deadly anger growing in Cheltenhamshire's citizens. The divorce rate was soaring—employees couldn't wait to get to work each day and night. It was better than scanning the airwaves for the 7,000 different words for 'bomb'.

The Director of GCHQ was a cross between a knighted Paddy Power and M. He made the Wolf of Wall Street look like Ba Ba Black Sheep. Each morning the knock came at his door signalling the arrival of the previous day's trading results marked 'eyes only', brought to him by a sort of executive casino pit manager.

"Come in."

"The figures, sir."

Sir Paddy, feet crossed on his desk, tilted back his croupier's hat, adjusted his silver Cartier sleeve armbands then riffled a pack of playing cards before taking the figures.

"Nothing like an invasion of a sovereign territory to boost our figures," he said, casting his eyes over the soaring military manufacturers' share prices.

"How is that miracle cure for baldness looking from Foliclepharma?"

"They will be announcing it next Friday, sir; we have placed a large amount of action on the stock."

"Excellent—and about time—getting a bit thin on top myself. This is the best news since Viagra. Any news on which company the Yanks are placing their new Wonderliner aircraft engine order with?"

"Staying with Uncle Sam, sir."

"Bastards! Buy their stock anyway. The name of the new royals' child?"

"It's twins, sir."

"Better odds! How's the Foreign Exchange div getting on pinpointing the next country to deliberately devalue their currency?"

"It's us, sir."

"Don't those tossers at the Bank of England know how much my family enjoy our European holidays? The World Cup bid?"

"FIFA, even by their standards, have surprised us on this one, sir."

"Talk to me."

"The newly formed Republic of Articis."

"Temperatures don't get above minus ten in the summer!"

"It's a done deal, sir—the reindeer economy has been replaced with the oil economy as the polar ice caps recede. The Eskies—the nascent national football side are naturals; they recently beat Brazil 3-0 in a pilot friendly match."

"You're forgetting we bet on that match and the Brazilian goalkeeper lost a finger to frostbite!"

"There is some good news, sir: the monopolies and merger commission will be declining the Wonkabury Chocolate merger."

"Makes you proud to be British. What about the banks, Satan bless them? We can normally rely on that nest of vipers and rattlesnakes to sow the seeds of the next scandal for us to reap."

"Clean as a whistle, sir; they seem to have used up the store cupboard of skulduggery."

"Bollocks! What team's working in that sector?"

"Red team, sir."

"That's the same crew that did our brains betting on the colour of the Queen's hat at Royal Ascot. Women always change their mind at the last bloody minute! Change the wheels on the car."

"Yes, sir."

"Did I tell you we're bringing back Seaweed and Troy from retirement?"

"No, sir."

"The most popular 90s act in Vegas; they've agreed to do a matinee and evening show, we have to spend the money on something—the troops will love it. Make sure you get the 'Gitts' front-row tickets."

I should mention at this point another well-known secret that had passed into fact lore—we had been conversing with aliens, aka the 'Gitts', for over 37 years.

The known story began on 19 August 1977, just after supper one Ohioan summer's evening. Dr Jerry Ehman turned up voluntarily to work on a S.E.T.I. (Search for Extra-Terrestrial Intelligence) project at the Big Ear radio telescope just south of Delaware. While routinely scanning the latest lottery batch of radio wave data his numbers came up. He detected a narrowband signal spike 30 times the level of normal interstellar space noise lasting for 72 seconds. It was the strongest signal ever to be seen before or after. On the original printout Ehman wrote 'Wow!' with red pen in the margin next to the circled numbers and letters. This became known as the famous 'Wow!' signal.

The signal was coming from the direction of a star group in the constellation Sagittarius near a star called Tau Sagittarii. All attempts to locate the signal again have failed, shrouding the 'Wow!' signal in mystery.

The explanation for its mysterious disappearance was simple. The original signal had come in at 10.16pm on 15 August, two days before Ehman had discovered it. That's the trouble with volunteers: you can never get enough of them to cover all the work.

GCHQ had no such problem. At 2.16am on Saturday 16 August 1977 PC (Pre-Casino), a junior scientific officer intercepted the signal and deciphered its code before breakfast and leaving his shift. During the handover he routinely informed his supervisor that he had asked the aliens to switch to a more secure frequency. Back then the spirit and embers of Bletchley Park still glowed. It was all in a day's work.

Sagittarians love travelling, which is just as well because they were about to make a round trip from the centre of the Milky Way to Earth some 130 light years away. The fun-loving Sagittarians and the boffins at GCHQ had been tweeting each other for more years than the Gitts cared to remember. Now, given the ability of the average GCHQ genius to fur the arteries with boredom and induce sudden cell death through conversation alone, the impression the Gitts had of the Earth was that it was not a place to kick off your alien shoes and let your hair down— if they had either. For three decades the Gitts chose to take up the invitations of other, more interesting, civilisations living in the galaxy. Now, like a long-distance pen pal, they were finally, out of politeness, dropping in to the heart of the Cotswolds and that doughnut of iniquity for a visit they weren't entirely looking forward to.

Meanwhile, back in Wellington Square, a car had pulled up. On the passenger seat was a copy of *Cage & Aviary Birds* opened on the classifieds page with a red circle around an advertisement. A barely visible woman emerged carrying a cage covered over with a blanket. She whispered a secret greeting through an entry door microphone:

*Close the door*
*Hit the floor*
*You never know who's in the corridor*
*Now we are ready to explore*
*Tell me more.*

# DUSKY THRUSH

There was a Regency townhouse smack bang in the middle of the Eastern approaches that looked like an enormous four-tier sponge wedding cake. It was decorated with classical fluted columns, scrolled capitals, cornices and modillions, all finished masterfully with buttercream icing. It made you want to break off a piece and eat it; even the chimneys looked delicious. Cheltenhamshire had a lot of wedding cake houses.

Within the top tier of the sponge cake, in his library overlooking the square, proudly sat Aloysius Gittler—the Chairman of the Cotswold Birding Society who was known affectionately by the members and his family as Louis. It was a closely guarded secret but Louis Gittler was shortly about to retire as the Head of Highways & Parking for Cheltenhamshire Council, after a lifetime of dedicated service. Gittler always described himself indistinctly as a civil servant.

Gittler was a pale man of below average height. He had a toothbrush moustache and brown hair with a side parting that he dutifully tended to ensure it remained permanently parted to the right side. He was dressed in standard-issue Chairman's uniform—flannelled trousers, white shirt and navy blazer with gold buttons. He was working enthusiastically on the preparations for his forthcoming retirement party.

Gittler was a keen amateur artist; his study was full of competent watercolours gracing the walls. Watching over him in joint pride of place next to a photograph of his wife and grown-up children sat his birding binoculars in a worn leather case. Suddenly, Gittler grabbed the binoculars from the case, hastily exiting the house at break neck evacuation speed in the direction of the communal garden as if a passing hungry giant no longer able to resist the mouth-watering cake temptation was about to cut himself a slice from Gittler's home.

It wasn't a hungry cake-eating giant. He had just received an anonymous email with a photo attachment of a rare dusky thrush perched happily in the turkey oak tree almost directly opposite his home. Panting deeply with excitement and lack of fitness, his trembling hands slowly adjusted the focus wheel to bring the dusky thrush into feathered focus.

"Oh my God! It is, it is!" Not since his father came face to face with a German Panzer division had those lenses seen such excitement (that is, putting to one side a brief, shameful period of voyeuristically watching a curvaceous woman undress each evening for six months in the Western approaches). He removed the binoculars from his disbelieving eyes to reveal a face of pure pale happiness. A dusky thrush on the doorstep of the Chairman of the Cotswold Birding Society—who would believe it? He felt like St Francis of Assisi—he knew that this mega bird event was his destiny; he'd been waiting for this one rare moment his entire life. He could see his picture adorning the front cover of *Birdwatching Magazine*.

"Think man, think!" said the patron saint of the dusky thrush to himself; there was so much to do. First he needed to report the bird, then he would set up a perimeter around the turkey oak; he would erect his marquee party tent as a temporary HQ in the garden for the invasion that was sure to follow. He had plenty of days holiday left that he could take. This would call on all his leadership and organisational skills; the birdwatchers' code must be followed to the letter. Gittler was in his element.

The twitching & birding community put International Rescue in the shade when it came to arriving on the bird scene quickly. The bird-vine professionally instigated by Louis Gittler had flown into action.

Thunder-Birders Are Go!

Hotel receptions went crazy with requests for room bookings; cars parked illegally all around the neighbourhood. They stormed the Garden Square carrying tripods and optical equipment. The bird brigade had evolved a unique gliding shuffle with their feet hardly leaving the ground—like a race walker to maximise speed and stealth, minimising noise and the movement of expensive equipment; they could carry their kit better than a Royal Marine Commando storming the beaches with a heavy machine gun. The average twitcher could be in position loaded and ready to fire quicker than the S.A.S. Any twitcher wishing to join Her Majesty's Armed Forces should be fast-tracked straight into combat.

Wellington Square was quickly besieged, occupied by a great army of bird lovers.

# APPALACHIA

In the autumnal lap of the White Mountains, New Hampshire, the sun had stained its reflection into the yellow and golden leaves of the aspen groves. Soon the leaves, unable to cling on, would let go of the tree's hand. The last orders of cool honeydew light had been drunk, giving way to dusk and the silhouette of looming spinal ridges. These old, now mortal Appalachian hills received the night un-sacrificed to mankind.

It travelled in the shortness of the day, in the cooling air, in the milky sperm of the Milky Way. It spoke from the breathing mouth of the white-bandaged bark, from its dark lenticel lips. It ran in its blood, in the taste of the breast-fed well sap and in the water from the creek. The cellular, pervasive urge to depart was upon the mountain when she was at her most irresistible.

This was now the wrenching hour, when with a magnetic force our juvenile yellow-bellied sapsucker would set-off from its arboreal woodpecker home on a maiden journey to a place it had never seen.

After a long spell that finally received its last incantation and blessing from the White Mountains themselves, they broke through the canopy, flapping into flock formation, a hundred-strong squadron of yellow-bellied woodpeckers flying over the elegy that was Appalachia.

Flying south by Orion's sword they passed directly over the home of the late poet Robert Frost. Such was the call of their new home they didn't even dip their wings in homage. A gentle 'me-aw' cat-like cry fell from their throats, dropping through the eaves onto his porch, untranslated into a Pulitzer Prize. Ironically, our woodpecker was about to take the 'road less travelled.'

Migration mission for Woody, our male sapsucker, was being accomplished as if he had written the manual himself, with the pleasure of a novice who was enjoying getting the hang of things. The manual sadly was about to be blown literally out of the sky. A vigorous fast-moving depression with westerly gale-force winds was about to disperse the flock, striking like a vengeful Stuka dive-bomber. Since the beginning, amendment-free, page one, the only page of the woodpecker migration manual read like this:

**Golden Rules:**
STICK TO YOUR LEADER LIKE GLUE
NEVER LEAVE YOUR WINGMAN OR WINGWOMAN
NEVER.

The propeller of wind quickly shredded the golden rules with the minimum of fuss. The sapsucker was dropped from the bird peloton, his cries for help unheard amidst the adrenaline and rushing wind. Alone, he frantically recalibrated his vector settings somewhere across the North Atlantic at 3,000 feet with a 65-mph tail-feather wind.

The turbulent air and the night sky in all its starlit storm-blown magnitude kept him company, as did the pale sun when eventually the morning came. His woodpeckery heart sank a thousand fathoms when that treeless sea with just the occasional shade of bilge green stretched on from horizon to horizon. All was sea. You cannot sup sap from the sea.

At first light on the third day a giant maple leaf a mile across from east to west appeared floating in the North Atlantic Ocean. It was a sign; it must be his winter home. He flew over the blind St Agnes lighthouse in the Scilly Isles whose light had long since been extinguished before circling and touching down in a small elm copse nearby. With his wings breathing a retracted sigh of relief he wasted no time tattooing the elm bark with his circular and rectangular calling-card wells. He licked and lapped at that tree bar like a thirsty dog, supping like he had never supped before; he belched with appreciation at that delicious British elm sap. It was without doubt the best sap meal that bird had ever tasted. Obligingly, the bartender set up another round of drinks—"On the house," said the elm tree, enjoying the company of this strange new customer.

# BARRY 'THE BIRDMAN' JONES

Barry 'the Birdman' Jones from the Rhondda, a controversial and legendary twitcher in the birding community, was not yet on his way to join the 'flaparazzi' in Wellington Square. The Birdman was a multiple 'year-lister' champion—the birdwatcher who saw the most species in a single calendar year—and was amongst the elite ranks of birders who had seen over 500 species in Britain.

Barry's successful scrap metal business did very nicely thank you very much, providing him with the financial means and time to fully pursue his obsession obsessively.

"It's either me or the Siberian blue robin," said his wife one evening, standing seductively in just high heels and stockings. She was no match for the extraordinary beauty of the Siberian blue. Birding bachelorism inevitably followed.

To be born in the Rhondda was to be born with mistrust and suspicion for outsiders buried deep in your heart (especially if they were from as far afield as Cardiff). Rhonddarian birthright conferred on them the boastful authority to chain talk stories on the marvelousness of themselves. Yet there was warmth, a hard-working loyalty, good humour and a rare strength of resilience and community that had against all the odds survived. Barry took these gifts of character and place proudly and confidently with him wherever he went. Not surprisingly Barry had a swagger that could rub people up the wrong way.

High tide had covered the tombolo sandbank between St Agnes and Gugh on the Scilly Isles, foolishly coming between Barry and his quest to list the yellow-bellied sapsucker, a mega-rare North American vagrant who had decided to temporarily leave the pub to do some sightseeing. With his clothes and paraphernalia lying in a heap on the beach, the Birdman strode towards the sea, his broad, squat frame giving him a rolling gait. He advanced towards the water with the purpose of a weightlifter approaching a bar. He had handsome olive skin with dark eyes—miner's DNA. Baldness looked well on him, as did the friendly mutton-chops about his face— there was something of the Victorian strongman about him. He stood wearing nothing but a pair of khaki shorts, dog tags around his neck and a parachute regiment tattoo on his right upper arm. On his left wrist he wore an Omega blue-dialled Seamaster GMT 300 Co-Axial watch favoured by the Special Boat Service. A man like that does not faff around with a cold-water tiptoe dance; he plunged in and with an efficient front crawl breathing every stroke was across to the island in no time at all, emerging as swiftly as a triathlete.

The Birdman was not called the Birdman for nothing. Like a fisherman who can stare into the running waters and see the trout lying in the current, or a detective who can see clues, the Birdman from wetlands to forests was the undisputed bird diviner. On this occasion he needed none of his supernatural powers.

He found the object of his quest looking out to sea, perched on the tilting nose of the Old Man of Gugh, a bronze-age standing stone—nine foot high and the colour of a grey whale. Woody tapped out a slow, moving Morse code on the head of the Old Man as if he was somehow delivering an ancient message. Perhaps it was a love message from an Old Woman menhir waiting loyally for him across the Atlantic.

With an excited sensory transcendence the Birdman meticulously conducted his identity authentication, inspecting and confirming his red head cap and throat, his barred black and white dress and the distinctive black bib and pale yellow breast wash. This was now officially the 400th bird he had listed that year. Each one had been like a tranquiliser soothing his soul, filling him up to the brim with security, protecting him; for this was something that nobody could take away from him.

There are dreams that are so vivid, so close to your inner desires that over time you come to believe they may have actually happened—they weave themselves into the fabric of your consciousness. They may be true, and if you look hard enough somewhere, someday, the evidence of their proof will present itself. Barry was in search of such a dream. A dream of emerald, gold and turquoise birds of such indescribable beauty they filled him with a deep peace. A dream he'd had a long time ago.

The elm bar was calling. The woodpecker alighted the craggy nose of the Old Man, still sniffing the salty sea, wanting to dive in and swim to his lover. Below him, Barry was already swimming back to the beach and his next adrenaline rush. His rare bird pager was bleeping with the hope of that dream in Wellington Square.

Waiting expectantly for the woodpecker's royal arrival was assembled some of the most sophisticated and powerful optical equipment money could buy.

In its Yankee homeland he was a modest creature, but here he was transformed into an almost mythical superstar by the fates of a fierce westerly wind. He wasn't carrying a message with the meaning of life; his shit did not cure cancer.

Behind each lens, every onlooker was a repository of life maps and charts, old and new. Seeing this vagrant bird was for many like briefly holding a magic compass.

From his very first heartbeat to his very last, Woody was never lost or lonely; from birth to death the master copy of him never changed, never became diminished or extinct.

Beyond the magnification of those instruments lay a far greater mega-rarity waiting to be discovered: the fearless glowing Appalachian blueprint of themselves.

# PETER, PAUL & MARY

*'Puff, the magic dragon lived by the sea and frolicked in the autumn mist in a land called Honnah Lee...'*

A sweet folk song sung by the 60's folk trio—Peter, Paul & Mary; a song of innocence with a sad ending and a firm favourite of the family by the same names living in Welly Square.

There was a time—let's call it 'the way it was' time—when Peter could lean his round cheek into his father's tender hands, when Peter would kiss him for his kindness, for understanding him so well. It was a time when Peter could just be a boy growing up, learning life's lessons, safely pushing the boundaries of behaviour where punishment was nothing more than being grounded, his tablet confiscated or an early bedtime, and where the judges felt guilty for their harsh sentencing and losing their tempers. The parental parole board ensured he never served a full sentence.

His tears would quickly dry to a dreamy boyhood sleep, never doubting the arrival of another happy day in the morning. This was the time when he felt safe and loved; when he could go to his dad for a hug and call his name, bursting with news of his latest adventures and achievements.

There was a time when Paul, his father, went through each day with unsullied pride in his son. He would find the energy to rise tired but enthusiastically from his armchair after a hard days work to the "Can we play?" call of boys—

wielding a lightsaber for an hour and winning an Oscar for best leading actor and sound effects. In the Garden Square Peter took his first wobbly ride on his bike, his parent's videoing and watching on with pride. They would kick and pass, bat and bowl, tackle and run, and practice catch after catch after catch in the Garden Square. "Make sure you keep your head still and cover the gap between bat and pad, like this." "Always tackle with your head outside their legs, like this." He would teach and play, teach and play.

The relationship Paul had with his son was his single greatest achievement in life.

There was a time when Mary, Peter's mother, watched both her boys with deep contentment. Each day she would produce little reassuring miracles: home cooked meals, fresh pyjamas for bed, correct school uniform laid out, packed lunches prepared, name labels sewn into kit, sunscreen applied or gloves and hat even when it was warm enough for a T-shirt—tender family apron strings.

It was a time when Mary and Paul still left notes for each other on the kitchen table signed with kisses. Paul loved to watch the way Mary efficiently grabbed her black hair, pulling it tightly before wrapping it skilfully around her fingers into a bun, then taking the pins from her mouth and fixing it to the back of her head. Paul would gently pull the pins out of that bun grenade in the evening and watch her hair cascade over her pale shoulders pretty as a flower opening its petals. This was a time when their hands still reached out with love towards each other. They still kissed with their mouths slightly open; they both wanted another child.

They would stand Peter up against the living room door to pencil mark his height. "Hey, keep your feet on the floor, you little monkey!" Together they would talk affectionately about him, their hopes and dreams, and see themselves in a smile, a yawn, and the shape of his body, his moles, freckles, the neckline and the eyes.

That was the sweet peace in time before Paul's business went bust. The time before he started gambling and drinking and paying for escorts. The lovely time before the shame and anger exploded into violence and a miscarriage.

Peter ran to help his mother, screaming and shouting at his father to leave her alone, with tears running down those cheeks; it was the first time he felt his father hit him. In that moment, everything Paul was most proud of dissolved.

During the summer holidays Peter began to build a protective cage for himself. He took control of his life with the help of an air-rifle and pellets that his father once used to shoot the vermin squirrels in the Garden Square. Laid out on the travertine paving stones of the back garden in species order were ten unburied corpses like a mini genocide; Peter admired them as if he were Buffalo Bill. The roll call of carnage read like this:

Magpies x 2
Female Woodpecker x 1
Blackbird x 1
Pigeons x 2
Song thrush x 1
Blue tit x 1
Robin x 1
Seagull x 1
If Puff the Magic Dragon had entered Peter's airspace

he would have killed him too. Some had died instantly; others, winged and crippled, had been executed as they tried to escape, pitifully flightless. The seagull came towards him, spinning and staggering like a stricken cowboy in a gunfight, before falling inches from his trainers. Peter liked this the best.

Peter threw the birds into the body bag of a black tie-up refuse sack and dumped them in the green wheelie bin before his father got home.

Mary was trapped; she still loved Paul. She was dreaming of a return to the family Land of 'Honnah Lee.'

Don't worry, folk fans, Paul had a plan. He was going to dig himself out of his debts and looming bankruptcy with one last massive bet. The assistant trainer to a well-known local training yard had given him the inside information on a 25–1 shot running at Cheltenhamshire on Saturday.

# THE CUCKOO OF AWARENESS (II)

"Stop now, Tom, please. Congratulations, that's a new meditation record, a full five minutes of total thought-free presence!"

"You felt how much I still miss my son at the very end when it broke down?"

"I did—it's your beautiful pain, Tom."

"It doesn't feel beautiful to me."

"Next time look at the pain—observe it. It is called love, Tom—it will never depart you. It's one of the most beautiful things I've had the honour to witness in my life."

"I'll try. At least you have been keeping my mind occupied writing the chronicles of Wellington Square."

"What do you think of its so far? A real page-turner in my modest opinion. You will hoover up all the non-fiction awards for history on the back of my hard work when this is over!"

"If you enjoy turning pages of painful autobiographical bleakness in the hope of finding more exciting pages of impending historical bleakness it's a must read."

"The pupil should always trust in the teaching methods of the Master!"

"My pen eagerly awaits you next dictated instalment, Master."

"Then I shall begin—"

"There has been one thing I've been meaning to ask you."

"Ask away."

"I've been wondering what you actually look like? Perhaps you'd like to reveal yourself to me in all your feathered splendour?"

"Unimaginably handsome, Tom."

"What does a handsome cuckoo look like?"

"A lot better than that retired salty sea dog—Rear Admiral Lunatic!"

"What a wanker he was!"

"A masturbator par excellence, Tom. When we talk together how do you imagine *moi*?"

"Well, this is where my imagination runs riot with originality—"

"I know what you're going to say, Tom, you picture me as the living embodiment of an immortal god wearing a golden crown, holding a sceptre, festooned in silken robes and precious jewellery, worshiped by legions of devoted loyal subjects?"

"No. I picture you as a slightly cocky name-dropping cuckoo that talks to me."

"Charming."

"So what do you really look like?"

"Rembrandt."

"He was no oil painting—if you will forgive the pun."

"You can see me, Tom, in lots of places."

"Like where?"

"Go to the National Gallery in London—Room 22—look for Rembrandt's *Self Portrait at the Age of 63*. When you find it, stare into his eyes, you will see me there. You will see me at the end of Verdi's *Requiem*, between the heavy silence and the applause; you will see me at first breaths, between breaths and last breaths; you will see me in the peace of quietude; you will see me when my song quickens the growth of all trees and plants and when, with increasing shades of soothing darkness, the wood puts the bluebells softly to sleep; you will see me in the fight and the surrender; you will see me in the still thusness of all things; you will see me at the centre of the hole in your heart, and you will see me most vividly when you see yourself."

"I'm glad I asked."

"Luckily for you, Tom, you will also see me - tomorrow."

"What about today's chronicles?"

"I'd like you to write up this little chat of ours please, Tom."

"Isn't it overly self-indulgent, having ourselves as authors in the chronicles? Can we not just stick to the historical events?"

"You mean author. You are, Tom, merely the writer, and not in the least—remember I am a 'cocky cuckoo' and you dear boy are a key witness who is very much part of the history and story of these great chronicles with every player having his entrances."

"I thought I was 'merely the writer', dear bird. It's the players exiting the chronicles I'm worried about!"

"We have indeed come a long way together with you now preferring to choose life over death."

"Seriously, we might need to consider taking a leaf out of the crow's book of sensible self preservation and leave this crazy neighbourhood pronto before whatever shit this is hits the fan!"

"I can guarantee it's shit of the highest calibre!"

"That's re-assuring."

"That's why this is no time for desertion, Tom.

Besides, I need my friend Sergeant Major Writer standing his war correspondent ground, shoulder to wing with me in the thick of the live recorded action."

"Your Cuckoo Needs You!"

"He does."

"Are you sure all these people and events are connected, anyway?"

"There is nothing random, Tom, all will become clear, I promise you. Enjoy the ride, as there is no running from your destiny."

"Only if you promise me more Wongo?"

"We've not heard the last of him."

"I'll be reporting for writing duty tomorrow then."

"You will particularly like the next chapter."

"Promise me it's not about me?"

"Promise."

# MOOM MONSTERS (I)

They didn't have a Latin name—like Dinosaur—
"terrible lizard" or Tyrannosaurus rex—king of the tyrant
lizards. Latin didn't exist to make them sound more real!
There was nothing tyrannical or terrible about the Moom
Monsters but they were just as real as terrible lizards! If it
did have to have the misfortune of being labelled with a
Latin name we would call it 'Magno Vento Comedenti,' for
reasons that will become clear later Freddie. Let us not get
ahead of ourselves the story is only just beginning!

Reassuringly, the fossilised bones of a Magno Vento
Comedenti or Moom Monster, have to this day never been
discovered. The curator of the natural history museum
would give their right elbow bone to get their hands on
one! Now, just because they were called monsters doesn't
necessarily mean they were big. If it did then they would
definitely be great monsters. They were big 'uns!

You might want to close your eyes now, Freddie, to
help you imagine. That's it. You have to imagine, son, for
the Moom is like nothing you have ever seen before. The
closest creature we have alive today for comparison is a
blue whale— but with some major alterations.

You could just about squeeze a Moom Monster onto a
Football pitch, if it breathed in. The pitch couldn't
accommodate its tail—that would have to stick out across
the touchline and down the players tunnel—the linesmen
or lineswoman would have to put up their flag for a throw
in! The width of a Moom's belly would be goal hanging in

both goalkeepers' goals!

Only if you had a seat in the very top tier of the stadium could you stare awe struck, mouth wide open, directly into their eyes. The Moom had two eyes, each as large as the searchlight light of a lighthouse or a stadium's floodlights. They were green and twinkly and full of kindness like yours. Let's call them kindness green. The arteries of a Moom were large enough for a small submarine to navigate and its heart was the size of a double decker bus—make that a triple decker!

Imagine the whale with the largest mouth—the bowhead whale; a giraffe could stand up in its mouth! Small fry. The mouth of the Moom could accommodate the largest tree on earth—the giant sequoia—as tall as Big Ben with just enough room to spare to pop on a top hat if it felt like showing off.

Next add an ear. Not a dinky little human ear like yours. The Moom had two large volcanic looking craters on their backs like Moon craters—one talking crater and one listening crater. The talking crater was much smaller than their enormous mouths for reasons we will discover later. They didn't have to worry about talking with their mouths full Freddie, as they had one for eating and one for talking! You can open your eyes now, but feel free to close them at any time if you sense the need for some extra imagination!

When it rained, the talking crater filled up with water, forming a small lake large enough for you to swim around in. You could slide down the rim of the crater like a water slide and splash land in the Moom Lake! It would be far too deep for you to dive down and touch the bottom! Mind you, I need you to listen very carefully as this is extremely important; do you hear me? You remember we told you never to go swimming in gravel pits or reservoirs because of the dangers? You now need to add a Moom Lake to that list. You don't want to be swallowed by a Moom, because that is what would happen if one opened their talking crater to take a refreshing drink. It was like a giant bath plug. You would travel struggling helplessly down the spiralling whirlpool towards their loud thirsty sucking lips at the bottom of the lake. The noise is ten times louder than grandma slurping her tea! Just like a black hole hoovering you up in space, nobody knows where you would end up once you passed the threshold of the Moom's lips and into the darkness beyond. Well I say nobody, never mind that for now.

If you were lucky, and it wasn't thirsty, it might blow you high up into the sky on a jet of water spume; you would then hold a world record for the highest water flume ride!

Now, just like you don't like getting shampoo in your eyes, the Moom didn't like getting fresh water in their ear craters. Salty seawater was no problem but fresh rainwater irritated their ears. Don't ask me why, I'm not a Moom doctor. At even the slightest hint of rain you would see them cover their ear craters by folding their large fluked tail backwards—like putting a lid on a gigantic saucepan. If you were brave enough to sneak up on a Moom to take a photograph, or God forbid, ask for a Moom selfie, the best time to do it would be when it was raining so it couldn't hear you coming!

A Moom standing outside our home in the garden of Wellington Square would cause a great eclipse of the sun, casting us into darkness, but don't be frightened Freddie, because the shadow of a Moom should not scare you...

# LAFONIA

**(Birthplace of Barry the Birdman)**

Charles Darwin was just a 24-year-old naturalist when on 1 March 1833 HMS Beagle dropped its anchor clattering to the seabed of Berkeley Sound, Lafonia.

His first impressions were telling: 'The land is low and undulating with stony peaks and bare ridges; it is universally covered by a brown wiry grass, which grows on the peat...The whole landscape...has an air of extreme desolation.'

With foresight and regret Darwin commented that the islands (Falklands) seemed destined to continue '...a bone of contention between nations.'

Lance Corporal Barry 'Taff' Jones of the 2nd Battalion, Parachute Regiment was just one year younger than Darwin when he lay slowly dying on a small patch of that contentious bone on the eponymous Darwin Hill. He would never see the view of the gentle plain rolling down into Goose Green afforded from its peak.

It was a foggy mid-morning in Lafonia. It sounded Swiftian. Lafonia—the land of the Lafonian's. It wasn't. Barry's platoon advanced up the slope of Darwin Ridge without the love of darkness for cover. They didn't have a dramatic cinematic Lafonic symphony gloriously accompanying them. They had their adrenaline and rushing young blood, sweat, skin and bones that loved ones would eat up, their humaneness, their excitement and fear, their pride and their training and a Darwinian instinct to survive. Military history and geography confirm factually that for most of that night they had fought an exhausting vicious frontal assault along a narrow isthmus.

Exposed perfectly for killing, a barrage without poetry of ferocious artillery, mortar and heavy machine-gun fire rained down on them from enemy trenches in a spur above them, lighting the fog with green and white tracer and overwhelming them, forcing them to retreat back to the entrance of the gorse gully from whence they came. Barry sensed the tall dark figure of his best 'butt' Stevie fall from behind him like a heavy shadow. By the time he had reached him the radiant light had gone from his young face; he'd had time for too many thoughts before dying, crystallised in a last warm precious tear on his cheek: a tear that spoke of his 3-year-old daughter—*who would love her and watch over her like him*? He briefly fought death not for himself but for his family: he saw their pain and felt their love, wished he'd written more in his letter home—died scared of dying, scared of dying for them.

Barry loved to stand by his side, basking in his bearish shade; a force of nature quickly spilling shit-talk and tales, crack of magnetic force. Barry kissed that tear from his face, kissed his unripened life, then hurriedly unclipped his webbing belt and removed his ammunition.

As he turned to retreat further down the gully, a mortar shell exploded just a few feet away. The rain-softened ground did its best to tenderly absorb the worst of the explosion, mixing muddy peat into the shockwave and shrapnel fragments that struck the back of his body. With the last vestiges of adrenaline, Barry instinctively crawled to his dead friend for shelter, their heads now resting side by side on thick grassy hummocks for pillows.

Stevie could not hear the percussion of blood and bodily fluids singing in Barry's brain. Barry's battledress had been torn to zombie-like shreds and for a short time he felt the hot water bottle of the earth warm him before realising it was his own blood seeping from him, transfusing into the blotting grass. His breathing was becoming heavy and laboured. The small fold of earth where they lay was like a tiny blanket unable to tuck them comfortably into that hill warmly and safely. It was close to freezing. When he was a child Barry used to sneak into his twin sister's bed, scared of the dark, scared of being alone, and now he was in bed again frightened, this time with a dead brother.

Unable to move and shaking with cold he could just feel the welcome, nearby heat of a gorse fire and smell the blue white smog of smouldering wood-smoke that was in plumes across the landscape. He could not hear it crackling above the freight trains, thuds and thunderclaps of acoustic death.

The gorse loved to burn—to die in a shindig of fire—it was delighted to die. It lay on its back puffing out smoke like it was leisurely smoking a large Havana cigar—a happy Wicker Man—knowing it would be re-incarnated and regenerated.

The wind loved to blow, but it was a bad posting for the wind, that treeless land. The paras relieved its boredom—tugging at them persistently for company—whispering to them to take it home like a Thai bride where it could sleep. They took a lot home.

Those days became like a cinematic memory fridge that would open many times. It was always well stocked and grew a little each year: acrid gun smoke, lashing rain, the smell of lanolin and almonds, belonging, gallows humour, fear, guilt, phosphorous, garlic, faces, fire, anger...each survivor had their own personal inventory in that fridge that would never defrost, never reach its expiry date. The fridge would offer up alcohol and say: "Here you go fella, this will make you feel better."

Around the boys an opportunistic spray of bullets in search of flesh entered the soft embracing belly of the earth without bleeding. He felt Stevie's body twitch, receiving them as sacrificially as a loving father for his son.

Barry had been lying for over two hours leaking blood and was now slipping in and out of consciousness. All around him was fading; atoms were departing the world of objects like souls, leaving behind lightness and fragility. If there was a sun in that cold-blooded sprat sky he could just reach out and pull it closer for warmth before eating it. He began to drift into happy thoughts of his family, of his sister Rhiannon and the stories his grandfather told them of her enchanted birds, who with the sweetness of their songs could awaken the dead and heal the sick and wounded. He could sense the battle raging again now with more intensity—*Go on lads, go on my beautiful boys, go on my red devils*, he thought proudly. As the tumult faded, three birds of the most exquisite beauty appeared to him like angelic sirens of emerald, gold and turquoise, filling him with a deep peace. Blindly, he found his dead friend's hand as the birds of Rhiannon began to sing him sweetly to sleep like an adagio of melted Welsh choir hearts.

A medic arrived, whistling nervously to himself the regimental quick-march 'The Ride of the Valkyries'. 'Quack' had seen too much already for his mind to ever forgive his eyes for having to try and forget. The sight of his two comrades holding hands would somehow mercifully endure above the butchery, always moving him to tears.

"Sorry I'm late, Taffy, don't worry, I'll have you back sheep shagging in no time," he said as he calmly began administering field dressings, morphine, saline and antibiotics. Like a Valkyrie, Quack had come to take the slain from the battlefield, but unlike them he had earthbound para wings and he wasn't leaving behind the living. Stretchers were in shorter supply than ammunition, reclining somewhere on leave, unstained. Instead, Taff was conveyed from the battlefield in a requisitioned wheelbarrow to the regimental aid post, where a helicopter would take him to the field hospital at Ajax Bay.

Flown by beautiful birds, the helicopter lifted into a Lafonian sky; the doctor heard Barry mumbling, "We are flying, Stevie we are flying..."

# WONGO THE WONDER DOG (II)

Wongo and the unknown poet were halfway through their afternoon walk around the perimeter of Cheltenhamshire Racecourse, a well-known walk for local dog walkers. It was day one of the two-day October 'Showcase' meeting, the first meeting of the national hunt season. It made a change from their ritual walk around the Garden Square and provided Wongo and his master an opportunity to enjoy the spectacle and sniff in its atmosphere without paying for entry.

The unknown poet pulled up Wongo at a large English oak tree, which marked the turning point for home. He stared wistfully up at its branches. Wongo followed suit, hoping there maybe some juicy squirrels he could get his teeth into. Last summer a stunt kite had its stunts well and truly stunted when it became tangled up in the highest branches of the oak tree. The kite knew the risks it was taking throwing caution to the wind. The tree had reached out and grabbed it with one of its tentacles, like a spiteful octopus covered in seaweed.

For three consecutive walks the unknown poet watched the helpless hostage suspended like a bauble, hanging like an invading storm kite paratrooper waiting to be cut down. At the unknown poet's mercy was an open poem goal and he fluffed it. On the fourth day the kite had either been rescued or escaped. More than a year later the kite poem still remained unconsummated. His poetic impotence was the source of much self-criticism: "If you can't convert these guilt edged opportunities you don't deserve to call yourself a poet!" The tree stood as a permanent memorial of his failure. Every time he passed by the failure he stared up, hoping that the kite would one day return like a mega rare migratory bird to roost in its upper branches and give him a second crack at writing a poem. It was a poem no-brainer that kept on wanting to give; the unknown poet noticed that the tree had fallen ill and was now dying. Its upper foliage was prematurely more thinned out than usual and paler in colour—it was dying from the top down. It was as if the kite had exacted its revenge by cursing its kidnapper to a long, lingering death.

Fortunately for the tree, God intervened, blasting the tree with a merciful lightning bolt and putting it out of its misery. The tree now looked like a tree ghost: white as skinless bone, whittled smooth by death. During the dark winter months the moon exposed the branches like a beautiful x-ray.

Wongo took his master's day dreaming contemplation as a clear signal for some playtime and promptly pulled the lead from his distracted hand and ran off dragging it along with him—hearing and ignoring with perfect deafness his increasingly loud master's commands, "Wongo! Wongo! Wongo!"

# OPERATION COLUMBO

Cheltenhamshire Football Club was no different from any other football league club. All known universal laws of model governance, boardroom behaviour & corporate responsibility enjoyed a large degree of footballmatic immunity:

"Now, before we discuss the appointment of a new manager, let's begin with the exciting matter of Operation Columbo."

"Operation *Colombian*, Mr Chairman."

"Yes, that's it, what's the latest?"

"We have conducted our due diligence on Mr Estevez and I am pleased to announce that apart from the usual suspicions of heavy involvement in match fixing, prostitution, money laundering, people trafficking, narcotics and gun running, I see no reason why we cannot sell the club to him today."

"I can hear the panpipes of the big time playing."

"There are some conditions, Mr Chairman, that Mr Estevez is insisting upon."

"Go on."

"The team shirts and colours will be changed to yellow, blue and red stripes and the club will be renamed Cheltenhamshire Condors Football Club."

"I like it—soaring over the Cotswold escarpment and up to the Premier League; the man is not only filthy rich, he is a marketing genius!"

"We will have to change the mascot, Mr Chairman."

"Not before time, mascots are supposed to bring us luck!"

"The Cotswold Condor?"

"Yes! Whaddney the Robin, our friendly national bird, has become a necessary victim of globalisation and been devoured by the condor, gentlemen, a far more stately bird."

"Come on you Condorrrrrs!" chanted the club secretary.

"We better get onto the Master Guild of Mascot Costume Makers quick for some designs," said someone wisely planning ahead.

"Where do I sign?"

"Just here, Mr Chairman."

"With the long-term future of the club safely secured, let's turn our attention to the vacant manager's position—any suggestions?"

"The local press is pushing the claims of Joe Hawthorne, following the tremendous success of the academy."

"It worries me he doesn't chew gum," said the Chairman, chewing heavily on his gum. "Shankly, Paisley, Clough—they didn't chew gum for nothing. We would be taking one hell of a chance on him."

Other board members chipped in:

"He's a posh bastard."

"Granted, he is very well spoken and polite but you can't argue with his success," said a voice of reason.

"We all know refs and linos respond well to verbal dog's abuse, many of them are addicted to it like a black moth to a flame—our opponents would gain an unfair advantage over the men in black if we didn't match them profanity for profanity."

"Excellent point—a moderate disposition is like a 10-point deduction."

"I've never heard him blame officials for his rare defeats—scapegoating them is our number one defence against the spotlight of blame falling unjustly on us."

"Number two, sacking the manager is the number one."

"He's very intelligent, name me one good thing anybody intelligent has done for football?"

"He would not be the fans' choice."

"Gentlemen," interrupted the Chairman, having heard enough.

"Thank you for your wisdom on this matter—but despite the huge success of the academy, we cannot ignore Hawthorne's complete lack of suitability for the post of manager. The runaway candidate is the local footballing legend that is Robbie 'Red Card' Monk."

"Mr Chairman—Red Card is in rehab for anger management."

"Precisely: by the time he gets out, he'll be like Mother Theresa! I therefore propose that we give Hawthorne a four-match contract as caretaker manager while the king-in-waiting awaits his coronation. All those in favour? Carried unanimously; any other business?"

"Yes, Mr Chairman."

"Let's hear it."

"Sombreros."

"Come again?"

"Sombreros for the club shop; the fans will love them, it's the iconic symbol of Colombia, it will make Mr Estevez feel at home."

"Buy big and airfreight them—I want every fan wearing their sombrero with pride at this week's match—the scarf has been living on borrowed time, I want to see our sombreros waving out of car windows."

"We should take advantage of the catering opportunity, Mr Chairman."

"I'm ahead of you—we can give the fans a culinary upgrade, the burger and pie van is dead, long live the burrito and enchilada van."

"Mr Chairman, those are Mexican, not Colombian foods—barbecued guinea pig and roasted ants are more to their taste."

"Get the marketing team to look at it—we need to do for guinea pigs and ants what sardines did for pilchards!"

So it came to pass that Joe Hawthorne, academy manager, toff, and life-long supporter, was promoted to take the reins of Cheltenhamshire Condors Football Club.

# JOHN DENVER

John Denver's groom was leading him around the parade ring. At 17 hands he was a lovely big chestnut colt. The local trainer informed the well-known owners and property tycoons, Mr & Mrs Whitechapel, they had just won best turned out, a lucky portent.

Mr Whitechapel smiled at the news but didn't give a shit about winning best turned out—*it's not a fucking fashion show* he thought to himself.

Benjamin Whitechapel—also known as 'Benny the Twitch' was a professional gangster in the grand manner. He was the east end boss of a well-organised criminal empire that was rapidly catching up with his good friend Mr Estevez. Unlike Mr Estevez, Benny preferred a less diverse portfolio of business interests; he stuck with what he knew best—narcotics.

Benny the Tic would have been a more medically accurate description of his habit of shrugging both shoulders simultaneously and involuntarily. The shrug would speed up and increase when he got nervous, excited or angry. Like all good gangsters he got angry a lot.

John Denver was named in memory of his late father's favourite singer. Benny's father—Geoffrey 'Glass Eye' Whitechapel—who, unlike his son, 'The Twitch', was given a 100 percent accurate gangsters handle by the naming panel of the time. Back in the day they had a little more class.

Mr Whitechapel cherished the memory of John Denver

winning his first bumper race at this very course and returning to the winners enclosure to the strains of "take me home country road..." from the happy punters.

Since then, John Denver had spent two seasons running with the handbrake mostly on. He had been plotted up for an almighty gamble—dropping down the handicap nicely.

At the last minute, the trainer had fortuitously and conveniently secured the services of the champion Irish jockey, as the original jockey booking became suddenly unwell. The going was perfect—good ground—the trip of three miles would play to his stamina. Timeform wrote in the race card: 'Very disappointing after promising start to career, others preferred'. None of the morning papers tipped him and he was friendless on the early morning betting exchanges. That was until the pre-orchestrated avalanche of money had backed him into evens favourite from 25-1. Fortunately for the trainer and the leaky assistant trainer, Benny the Twitch had got all his considerable bets on John Denver to win at very decent prices.

Mr Whitechapel went into a pre-race huddle with the trainer and jockey wearing the familiar all white silk colours of the owners. The same colour as the devastating powder that he infected the streets with. The trainer issued clear instructions to keep John Denver handy out of trouble, scraping paint on the inside rail for the first circuit before taking it up in front of the grandstand for the final circuit. Benny the Twitch had just a few words of motivational encouragement for the jockey as the bell rang for the horses to leave the parade ring and head out to the start.

The Twitch placed two large sweaty paws on the slim shoulders of the jockey, smiling and shrugging his excited large shoulders before giving him some fatherly advice:

"The bread and honey is daahhhn, I dann't care if ya 'ave ter whip the Brad Pitt aahht of him, or carry 'im over the line, just win!" He gave the bemused jockey's chiselled cheeks a gentle twist before giving him a leg up, then, with great decency and perfect queen's English, shouted to the jockey—"Come back safely," loud enough for his wife to hear him before heading off to the owners and trainers section of the stand to watch the race.

Everything was going to plan, John Denver was travelling supremely well, he hadn't touched a twig, he'd jumped the tricky third last and the jockey was oozing confidence, looking over his shoulder and between his legs for rivals that were already rowing away in behind him off the bridle. He hadn't moved a muscle; John Denver was still on the snaff and looking like the proverbial steering job. The trainer was rehearsing his exculpation speech to the stewards following the inevitable enquiry that would follow as to John Denver's dramatic improvement in form. The only danger to him not winning now was if some space hardware fell from a satellite, re-entered Earth's atmosphere and crashed into horse and jockey. This was the prayer of on-course, online and high street bookmakers whose liabilities were pretty astronomical: they would need to be taken out on a stretcher if John Denver won.

All their prayers were answered in the wondrous form of Wongo the Wonder Dog. Wongo sped onto the track, easily avoiding the stewards—using his whippet speed to good advantage in his quest to introduce himself to John

Denver and the white elf sat on top of him. Despite coming to meet the second last on a perfect stride, Wongo's sudden appearance at his hooves spooked John Denver into putting down on his jockey to crashing and catastrophic effect with the race at his mercy.

The stunned champion jockey managed to sit up nursing a broken collarbone, meanwhile a quick witted steward was frantically waving a white flag to direct the remaining horses and riders around the fence where John Denver was lying stricken on the other side. Wongo was jumping up with excitement, licking the face of the incandescent champion leprechaun who then got to his feet and kicked Wongo in the head with anger. Later the R.S.P.C.A. would investigate this cruel brutality caught on live television and the on-course TV screens.

Wongo returned to his owner, who was completely oblivious to the carnage he'd caused—"Good boy, Wongo, there's a good boy," he said, patting him and making a fuss over him, unwittingly condoning Wongo's murderous antics. Even Wongo thought he was in a spot of bovver, which is why he returned to his master for the first time in his life.

Benny the Twitch witnessed the scene partially from behind his binoculars; his twitch was so out of control that his binoculars spent a large amount of time being viewed by his forehead. A black screen had been erected around John Denver; a bolt gun was pointed to his skull. John Denver would not be taken home down country roads to the stable he belonged. He was not leaving on a jet-plane. By the time the owners got there he was already in the horsemeat wagon.

One or two bookmakers enjoyed some good publicity

by refunding bets on the losing favourite. The independent bookie that took Paul's bet didn't. The police had to be called from the bookies to drag him out ranting and raving.

# SITTING BULL

Bob 'Sitting Bull' Brady or, as he was less well known, Dancing Bob or Wayward Bob, was crazy with undiagnosed craziness. Bob would need industrial grade lagging for a cell rather than padding. If Bob Brady played in the World Series Poker final for the unhinged they'd be folding their bananas and handing over their jelly babies after Bob had raised their wackiness and doubled it. His madness would be too rich for their blood. Bob was the nutter's nutter.

He had always been unconventional but he was now taking it to a whole new level. He was living a full and normal crazy life: a life that was far fuller and colourful than the life he lived as a sane man. His appearance was similar to the face of the Shroud of Turin; he still had more blonde hair then grey in his beard and moustache. Craziness preserved him; crazy people don't worry.

Bob stared intently at a parked car from the sash windows of his top-floor flat overlooking the square. The automobile was perfectly parked equidistant between the residential parking grids. Insured, taxed and perfectly parked, minding its own metallic business, glistening as it sunbathed in the sun. Bob was trying to levitate the car with the power of his mind. He was ambitious—preferring to start big rather than with matchsticks. He could have begun with the small Mini parked behind it, but no, he had set the levitation bar at a world record weight for his first attempt and was confidently tackling a 4 x 4.

Bob believed he was born with special powers and using them just took concentration and practice. He had yet to find the willpower to give up smoking, cannabis and pornography. The car didn't feel the slightest bit uncomfortable; it couldn't sense him staring or feel its molecular cells tingling with kinetic energy. It stubbornly resisted his mind.

His intentions were admirable, good ones—he just wanted to pick up all the cars parked in Wellington Square with the power of his mind and dump them one by one into the reserved parking spaces marked for the council's elite Highways & Parking Team. He hadn't worked out whether he would just lay them down gently in the middle of the car park or pile them on top of parked cars; he would worry about that once he got them airborne.

Bob had carsickness without being in a car. He was sick of looking at them, seeing them constantly, hearing them wake and watching them sleep. He even hated the way they moved, limbless, graceless, unlike the fox or the jumping badger. They all wore black tyres like an evil army. He wanted to liberate the square from the black tyres and bring peace to his mind.

Bob had form when it came to cars. Due to its quiet location, the square was a haven for learner drivers and driving instructors who understandably exploited this weakness for their own advantage. It was like Heathrow airport on a busy day with cars in a holding pattern in different parts of the square waiting for clearance to practice their three point turns and reverse parking. Eventually, a man with Bob's constitution was going to crack. He'd already cracked so the crack was just going to get worse.

Last April Bob was returning home carrying two white plastic bags full of shopping, wearing a white shirt. The white shirt is an important detail because it's similar to the white shirt 'Tank Man' was wearing when he stood in front of a Chinese tank column in Tiananmen Square Beijing waving his unknown shopping items at the tank commander in an attempt to bring freedom and democracy to China whilst gunfire rang out all around him. That was a hell of a day for the young man; one moment he was looking forward to getting home and eating the wontons and sweet and sour pork he had just picked up at the local store, the next he'd climbed on top of one of the planet's most deadly machines to plead with the Chinese army to go back to their barracks and leave his people in peace.

Bob took a leaf out of Tank Man's book and decided to make a stand for the democratic freedoms of the residents when he blocked a learner driver with L-plates, who, without dual controls, was floundering in the middle of the road. Every time the car tried to move, Bob stood in front of it, waving his shopping up and down like Tank Man. The passenger wound down the window, mindful of his young daughter at the steering wheel.

"What's your problem, mate?"

"Tired of learner Iron Horses ruining our homeland," said Bob, still moving the shopping up and down like the paddles used to direct an aircraft.

"You're of your head fella," said the passenger, hitting the nail firmly on the head. Bob quickly confirmed the diagnosis:

"You insult my people by driving Jeep Cherokee," said Bob, sitting down and taking a can of lager from his shopping bag and opening it.

A queue of driving instructors was now waiting to land in Wellington Square, along with a few residents who were caught up in the congestion, their patience being slowly bled dry. It was not long before Bob's brand of crazy magnetism attracted the sympathies of frustrated residents who soon willingly joined him sat in the road. Never missing an opportunity for self-promotion the PEOPLE AGAINST BUREAUCRACY (PAB) councillor rapidly arrived on the scene carrying his election board full of solidarity for his voters. It was another two years before the next election but he never went anywhere without his sign. Only last week he'd arrived in casualty to seek out a swing voter of his ward who had broken her ankle on the uneven pavements—something his manifesto would have prevented if only she had voted for him. Eventually the police were called to bring the protest to an end but not before enhancing Bob's burgeoning reputation as a man of the people.

The dusky thrush had been bringing fresh cars into the square on a daily car tide making Bob madder than normal. The local residents regarded Bob as an amusing eccentric, a rebel renegade raging against life's mores and a corrupt and inept local government. He was the antidote to the banality of their walking corpse lives.

They had no idea how badly the craziness was fucking him up. He was not eccentric: he was a madman.

# W.S.R.C

Bob was the self-appointed leader of the Wellington Square Residents Committee (WSRC). The committee's responsibilities included: protecting the square's unique architectural character, closing down Guantanamo and defeating the council's notorious crack Highways & Parking Team, the Neighbourhood Watch scheme, organising street parties and the annual leaf clean-up, dinner safaris and swinging events.

Sitting Bull and his resident braves were on the warpath. The previous evening they'd gathered at the grand regency villa of Laughing Bear that occupied a large plot of land in the western corner of the square. Bob had given all the committee members' Native American Indian handles. Each member of the committee was highly deserving of lengthy character development. Actually they deserved much more than the artifice of clever description. These were real people after all, where reality means nobody ever really knew the secret lives of anybody (unless of course, you are the omniscient Cuckoo of Awareness) and no amount of description was ever going to change that.

During the 1860s the great novelist and clever describer, Charles Dickens, regularly visited 6 Wellington Square to see his dear friend and the most famous Shakespearean actor of his day—William Charles Macready (1793–1873). Today a bronze tablet commemorates his residence here from 1860–1873, where he spent his retirement and lived out the last years of his long life. The celebrated poet Alfred, Lord Tennyson dedicated this sonnet to him.

To W.C. Macready

## By Alfred Lord Tennyson

1851

Farewell, Macready, since to-night we part;
Full-handed thunders often have confessed
Thy power, well-used to move the public breast.
We thank thee with our voice, and from the heart.
Farewell, Macready, since this night we part,
Go, take thine honors home; rank with the best,
Garrick and statelier Kemble, and the rest
Who made a nation purer through their art.
Thine is it that our drama did not die,
Nor flicker down to brainless pantomime,
And those gilt gauds men-children swarm to see.
Farewell, Macready, moral, grave, sublime;
Our Shakespeare's bland and universal eye
Dwells pleased, through twice a hundred years, on thee.

Dickens should have visited over 150 years later. The cast of the WSRC would have replaced the ham actors of Mr Bumble, Miss Haversham, Uriah Heep, Fagin, Samuel Pickwick and Nancy.

Let's take our host by way of an example—Laughing Bear, aka Dave Chalkley or 'Chalk' to his friends, a retired vet and animal lover. A decent homo-sapien highly deserving of a certificate recognising his contribution to the human race. On the face of it Chalk was a swell guy, a man you'd be honoured to call your friend. On the face of it, yes, but under the face of it, he was secretly flawed. Everyone has a flaw or two and Laughing Bear was no different to every normally flawed person. Nobody is interested in flawlessness, so let me get it over with and tell you what his secret flaws were. Let's put to one side his life: the messy divorce when the wife he adored ran off with another woman, the abortion—yeah all that life stuff and stuffing, let's put that to one side.

Chalk would spend a lot of time alone sat in his high ceilinged living room listening to kitsch jolly good news music from the 1950s, full of fast strings and brass instruments extolling the virtues of vacations and lifestyle. He had it on loop continuously; it was like being put on hold in incidental music land. Most folk would hang up after a few minutes but not Chalk. It seemed to act like a painkiller to the internal struggles going on inside him. The music helped him to block out listening to the bitterness of himself.

Friday was fish day, a special treat he looked forward to. Fish tanks are considered therapeutic by many and for Chalk it certainly proved to be the case. The aquarium he owned was a deluxe version. It was full of seabed furniture from sea furniture land. The fish were right at home and thought they had fallen on their fins. It was the Watership Down for fish. Chalk had divided the large tank with a glass wall divider. On the left of the tank were starved male tiger fish and on the right were well fed female guppies. Every Friday, Chalk would, like the good animal lover he was, get up from his armchair and pull up the glass drawbridge for the tiger fish to swim under; with his face almost touching the glass he watched with sadistic pleasure as the males ate the females to British Pathé newsreel joviality.

Laughing Bear's unknown flaw was made a lot worse when he decided that due to his hatred of women there was nothing else for it—he would become a gay man. He employed an unlicensed back street therapist willing to commence 'SCT'—Straight Conversion Therapy. His days as a straight man had brought nothing but pain to him. It was a botch job. The reconditioning experimentation with male-to-male love damaged Chalk almost beyond repair.

We just have time for one more quick WSRC character—Pantomime Pete. Pete was a flamboyant hairdresser who tried too hard to look younger than his half century and was a sucker for the latest weight loss fad. Pete loved panto. He was a permanent fixture on the local amateur dramatic panto scene—always playing a dame in drag. William Charles Macready would be turning in his grave, as would Alfred Lord Tennyson (*'Nor flicker down to brainless pantomime'*). Panto Pete longed to be a pantowright. For 20 years he'd tried unsuccessfully to put panto pen to paper. The industry was desperate for new jokes and subject matter to freshen up the traditional repertoire. He was currently working on a version of Sweeney Todd (Weanie Todger). He'd written over 20 panto scripts for stage and they'd all been turned down. Despite this, and to his great credit, he refused to get down in the panto dumps. Cheerfully, Pete continued to fasten his clients to the cliff face of his experimental pantomime jokes whilst styling their hair. They were lucky to get out with their sanity!

Bob addressed the gathered committee, or council of the elders, as Bob preferred them to be known. All were swollen in their united enmity towards the dusky thrush and Guantanamo, both of which were making their lives a living hell. The untimely death of a popular cat, 'Growl Tiger', mercilessly run over by a birder rushing to the square, had ignited passions further—"We all know how much these birders hate cats—it was deliberate murder to protect the thrush!" said the widow of Growl Tiger fighting back the tears.

All braves were present and correct. Like all great leaders, Sitting Bull knew exactly how to powerfully articulate what his followers wanted; he addressed the group, his braided hair draped over his shoulders; he was wearing a long feather war bonnet headdress, buckskin shirt, leggings and moccasins; he had a spray-on tan to complete his appearance. Like another former resident in William Charles Macready, Bob had the power 'to move the public breast'.

"I remember when the great Buffalo Tatanka roamed these lands in vast numbers before the white man came with his iron horses and lust for shining dust, destroying our plain's lifestyle. The Cheltenhamshire Grandfather has promised much. Instead, he gives us metal soldiers with hungry mouths, builds supermarkets we do not need, homes our people cannot afford, and worst of all he gives us Guantanamo! The Birder tribe have taken over our ancestral home, invading our reservation like our sworn enemy, the Crow."

The WSRC members were hungry for this kind of parley.

"We must fight back!" cried Little Big Man, inspired.

"Fight back," repeated Crazy Parrot.

"Death to the cat killers!" said the cat-less widow.

"Death to the Thrush!" chirped Many Husbands.

"Death to Guantanamo!" hammed Pantomime.

"Death to the Highways & Parking Team," said Laughing Bear, laughing.

"Death to the Crow!" said Window Licker.

"Death!" repeated Crazy Parrot.

"Thunder Thighs, do you still have good relations with the Great Paper Chief?"

"Yes, Bob."

"Great Paper Chief," repeated Crazy Parrot.

"We will arrange a heap big demonstration on Saturday afternoon with all our brave warriors and friends—invite their reporters and photographers."

"Heap Big demonstration," repeated Crazy Parrot.

The meeting proceeded efficiently to set the date for the annual autumn leaf clean up with Returns Home Late volunteering to organise the leaflets and Many Husbands offering to provide mince pies and hot drinks. Dinner Safari courses were oversubscribed with eager volunteers. The agenda tended to move very quickly at the WSRC meetings with a growing excitement in the loins long before 'Any other business?' Sitting Bull requested the keys of the willing committee members and placed them in his headdress.

"Don't forget tomorrow is National Give Up Pornography Day," he said with casual madness before drawing them out.

"National Give Up Pornography Day," said Crazy Parrot.

# MOOM MONSTERS (II)

Don't be frightened, Freddie, the shadow of a Moom should not scare you. Mooms were magical, friendly creatures.

You remember when we go to the seaside on holiday and sand seems to get into everything no matter how much you brush or wash it off? I bet we could still find some in our suitcases upstairs from our last holiday or even behind your ears! Well, sometimes sand getting into things is very valuable. Your grandma's pearl earrings were once a common grain of sand!

They were formed when a tiny grain of sand smuggled itself inside one of the two shells of the oyster. The oyster gets very irritated by the grain intruder. Oysters can't scratch the intruder itch; can you imagine what it must be like not to scratch that itch between your shoulder blades that Mummy or me get for you? Up a bit, left a bit, a bit more, yes, just there! Just there! Ahhhhhhh. Instead of hands the oyster scratches itself by painting the bothersome stowaway with many coats of mother-of-pearl, after a lot of licks of this paint the beautiful round iridescent gem is formed. That makes the oyster feel a lot better, Freddie. The Moom was a bit like an oyster; let me begin to tell you why:

At the same time every year—of years that have only survived in folklore—a great festival took place on a small island called Murria. Murria was twice the size of the Isle of Wight.

It took place when long wooden ladders scaled the orchard trees; the red and green apples were ready for eating, ready for the pie and for the cider press. Spiders were spinning their sticky crystal webs in search of faces to walk into them just for spooky laughs. Doddery wasps defied dying, surviving only on the dream of savage stinging spite. This same time every year tasted of blackberries and smelt of toadstools revelling in the dew— you would know them as mushrooms. A colder wind had begun stripping some of the trees of their clothing to reveal deserted empty birds' nests. Above them flew the birds, going on holiday to incredible places long ago forgotten that we will discover. It was autumn.

The climate of Murria was much milder than ours, Freddie; the people of Murria never saw snow, never had a snowball fight, built an igloo or made a snowman. If they did have snow I bet it wouldn't take the children long to work out what to do with the stuff!

Under the stars and the moon, giant turtles return to the same beach that they were born to lay their eggs. It's a wonderful magical sight to see them appearing from the gently fizzing foamy surf. They make their way up the beach to find a suitable spot of sand to dig a hole for their babies to be born in using their flippers like a spade.

The Moom were returning to Murria but not to lay eggs.

The men, women and children of Murria, known as the Mu, lined their great harbour wall. The French word for wall, Freddie, is *mur*; perhaps this was where the word originated. The harbour wall of Murria was one of the wonders of the ancient world. You could say it was a wonder wall! It could be seen from space long before astronauts and satellites looked down upon us. We are talking pre-space junkyard times, before pollution and asthma. You wouldn't have needed your inhaler if you lived in Murria, Freddie! Even on an island as small as Murria there were places untouched and undiscovered by humans. Nothing was yet on the edge of existence or survival. There were quiet beach coves where the sand had never felt feet, rivers that had never been fished or swum in, caves unexplored, forests never walked in, and where beautiful silences grew, nameless valleys and secret, strange places and the Mu knew that they were all better places for it. The Mu were just happy knowing they were there. This was a golden time.

At each end of the enormous horseshoe mouth of the harbour wall stood two magnificent lighthouses illuminating the sea; on the hillsides, great beacons lit the land. The Mu were feasting, drinking and dancing to music. Moom Festival merriment filled the blackberry night air.

There were no boats in the harbour. They were now safely anchored in the quiet west of the island. The Mu travelled to the great harbour by horse-drawn wooden caravans and carts, donkey and pony. The horses had been groomed and decorated as if they'd been to the beauty parlour. Their manes had been gorgeously braded with brightly coloured ribbons and flowers; their tack sparkled from polishing. Children rode on ponies and donkeys with their head collars, reins and saddlecloths all lavishly decorated with bright accessories of fabric. The Mu transportation was like a carnival float and prizes for best in class were hotly contested. Competition was fierce amongst the Mu women to be crowned the Moom Queen.

Everyone wore his or her best clothes. They were some of the finest garments ever made. All their clothes were made from sea silk—sea silk was even finer than silk, light as a feather and warm. Today, sea silk fabric is very rare and expensive and has been used to clothe Kings, Queens, Pharaohs and Emperors; the art of spinning it has almost died out.

Let me tell you a little known fact, Freddie. The word *mermaid* actually came from Mumaid. The Mumaids of Murria would dive into the warm bay of Murria to harvest the precious sea silk fibres that anchored the special clamshells to the seabed. You could say sea silk was made out of anchor rope! The Mumaid would have made a great synchronised swimming team: they could hold their breathe for four minutes! Let's see how long you can hold yours for tomorrow in the bath!

Once they'd spun the sea silk fibres they would then dye them with spices and the juice of Murria lemons. Not only did Murria lemons make the best lemonade and lemon meringue pie you've ever tasted, they also turned the sea silk a beautiful dark golden colour that never faded and glistened like copper when light touched it. From their looms the Mumaids wove gloves, socks, hats and robes; blankets, capes, scarves, stockings and bracelets, you name it—even pyjamas! The famous muumuu dress worn today by women was created centuries before by the fashionable Mu. If you're a good boy I will take you to the British Museum where you can see with your own eyes the only surviving link we have to the folk stories: a ladies right hand glove. On the inside is a label that says 'Made in Murria.'

All summer the people of Murria had been preparing

the hillside common that looked down upon their beautiful city with the most luxurious bed of straw you've ever seen. It was fit for a Moom to sleep and rest comfortably. The Moom would be checking into a five star hotel room.

# VISITATION

An elegant, regal-bearing woman in her mid-50s was door-knocking the residents of Wellington Square. She wore a powdery pistachio coloured coat with a thick waffle texture and an oversize collar where she sported a pretty jonquil flower brooch; it had 60s-style large buttons like macaroons and two small pockets at the front. The dress underneath was an A-line tunic in cream with a delicate print. Around her neck she wore a three-strand pearl necklace to match her pearl-button earrings and on her feet were comfortable black-buckle shoes; her hands were covered in brushed cotton white gloves. Her dark hair had a curly bouffant bonnet with the fringe backcombed off her forehead. Her makeup and lipstick had been applied delicately and tastefully. She carried herself with great deportment, moving with the fluidity of a far younger woman. She smelt of rose perfume and carried a black leather top-handled Diva handbag by Launer with its distinctive gold-plated rope logo clasp. Its silk lining had the matronly comforting smell of a peppermint factory— you could put your head inside that handbag and come out a better person. Residents were uncharacteristically opening their doors almost before the gate whined open with news of her arrival. "I'm from the council," she said fearlessly, without a trace of shame or embarrassment, flashing her Miss E Windsor photo identity hanging from her neck. "We are getting out in the community to make sure you are getting everything you need from us, is there anything I can do for you?" It was if she had brought back to life a dead relative or returned to them a lost child or pet. The lady from the council attracted none of the normal and thoroughly deserved splenetic projection and violent hostility of citizens who had suffered mercilessly at the fascist hands of the council. Public consultations were no more than a sham exercise in snarled lip-service democracy. Local residents were suffering from battle fatigue, tortured by stupidity, constantly banging their common-sense heads against a brick wall constructed and defended by an army of pygmies. They were on the verge of surrendering and laying down their weapons of community thoughtfulness, resigning themselves to the awfulising status quo, when this minty angel of hope with a pleasing, well-spoken manner appeared at their door prepared to work on a weekend. Hallelujah.

For many residents the encounter would become worthy of a new chapter in the King James Bible. Every visit followed a similar pattern: the ceremonial offer and courteous acceptance of a cup of tea (white, no sugar) which she never drank, after which she would sit with the presence of a female Buddha, totally at ease with herself. She had an enlightened presence.

As she sat down with perfect posture, Miss Windsor would open the gold clasp of her handbag—the front door to the peppermint factory. At first came the familiar grumbling refrain of personal vexations, grievances and defeated crusades: blocked drains that flooded and smelt, potholes, the mystery of the unrecyclable cardboard drinking cartons who were refused the recycling treatment they so urgently deserved, stone pavements replaced with blobs of tarmac, broken street lights, driving instructors, drug addicts and of course always, always the open festering wound of Guantanamo.

They all talked with the certainty in their hearts that this woman was going to fix everything, and then something extraordinary happened. Everyone she met began to confide in her exactly five minutes after her arrival—like a human poultice she drew out his or her most private feelings. Whilst the outward appearance of Wellington Square may appear cultured, tranquil and solidly middle class, the inward life of its residents was not always compatible with its surroundings:

"The cancer is back, I'm riddled with it, they can't do anything for me..."

"I've had six miscarriages, we want a child so badly..."

"Even now, ten years later, there isn't a day that goes by I don't regret the abortion..."

"He hits me and our son, I'm scared..."

"I'm a drunk..."

"I was adopted, abandoned by my parents..."

"I'm a fat cow..."

"I don't love him anymore..."

"I'm a heroin addict..."

"I hate my stammer..."

"Do you know what it's like to be a minority in this racist town?"

"I'm lonely..."

"Our son, Freddie, was only 13 when he was given the drugs that killed him..."

"I love my dog..."

They all cried, the young and old, they all cried into that perfectly tailored coat—it was as if it was harvesting the tears of the human condition. She held them crying;

they all felt like the arms of the universe were cradling them.

The only person not to open their heart and who was seemingly immune to her powerful presence was a man dressed as a Red Indian who went by the name of Sitting Bull. "Please come in," he said politely before adding, "You must be the virgin empress promised to me since the dawn of time." After five minutes, instead of revealing his deepest feelings, he asked her if she would like to see the 'Machine of Happiness' he had built, and lie with him naked in bed.

Door to door she went, and when she left, people felt better. Somebody had actually listened to them and understood them. Such was their gratitude, residents afterwards wrote, emailed and phoned the local paper and council, lavishly praising the council's new breath of fresh air initiative and the dedication of Miss Windsor; she should be knighted for her services. After decades of conflict and antagonism, hopes were raised that peace and reconciliation could usher in a golden age of public and council cooperation and harmony.

The council moved with totalitarian speed to stamp out the 'rumours,' denying both the existence of the initiative and of a Miss E Windsor ever working for them. The last thing they wanted was to actually get a reputation for listening to people, let alone working weekends. They even took out a front and back page advertising spread in the local newspaper with an artist's impression of the 'imposter' asking citizens to be on the look out for this dangerous hoaxer and even issued a 'Do not approach under any circumstances' warning.

The events of that day became shrouded in mystery.

Twelve months later, a local investigative journalist interviewed a handful of the 'visitee's' living in the square, all convinced that Miss E Windsor possessed remarkable healing powers. Her findings were miraculous: one woman told of how, after many miscarriages, she had fallen pregnant and given birth to twins; another of how her breast cancer had vanished—the doctors had never seen anything like it. A young man told of how each time he began the purposeful, curative ritual of cooking heroin a gentle voice began speaking softly inside his head. It spoke to the 11-year-old boy who had lost his father, it said: "I'm going to look after you—put it down, son." Every time he fired up his lighter the voice spoke. Hours turned into days, weeks into months of being clean. He did as he was told and never picked it up again.

# SCARLET LIGHTNING

Two days after the visitation a teenage girl woke up to the normal pre-school drill, which she conducted in reclusive silence, communicating with gestures rather than words. It was better that way: more relaxing for everyone without the face contortions and tension.

"Can you get the front door, darling?" shouted her mum, tied up with make-up. The parcel deliveryman was standing at the door, holding out his handheld patented germ-collecting device.

"Good morning, young lady, can I have a name, please?" Since the age of four she had not been able to speak her own name without stammering. Like all the other words, she knew exactly what she wanted to say and how to say it, she could picture every letter and syllable beautifully un-stammered, but her mouth and tongue would not cooperate with her brain. That was a shame, not least because she had a name fit for a movie star. Instead of the normal anxiety of a racing heart and sweaty palms in anticipation of humiliation, Scarlet Lightning just said "Scarlet Lightning".

"What a great name," said the deliveryman. "Sign here, please, in the box."

"Thank you," she replied without thinking. Just as the deliveryman was about to jump into the van to move at high speed onto his next microbe destination, she shouted after him: "Ask me my name again!"

"Sure, it's all part of the service; what's your name,

kid?"

"Scarlet Lightning, my name is Scarlet Lightning!" she said loud and proud, smiling like a movie star, before racing back into the house, shrieking.

# BASILICA

There were many more stories yet to be discovered from residents who were now re-writing the story of their new lives without sickness, alcohol or binging, without guilt or fear following their close encounter with Miss E Windsor.

Many residents, or the 'chosen ones' as they later became known, were keen to cash in on the publicity, just as many who had not been at home at the time also leapt on the miracle bandwagon. Eagerly, they gave press conferences and interviews, describing Miss Windsor as having an effulgent white radiance of beauty. The miracle bandwagon just kept on picking up divine speed. Catholics believed the residents had seen an apparition of the Blessed Virgin Mary. An apparition of this magnitude was long overdue and it ticked all the apparition boxes.

The Doughnuts playfully placed a full size cardboard icon of the Blessed Virgin Mary in the Garden. That didn't help.

Pilgrims pilgrimaged to the shrine.

They spoke of the special atmosphere and holiness of the place and gave it a 5 star spiritual review rating.

They came in greater numbers.

It was good for local tourism.

The visitee's gave lucrative talks and guided tours.

The religious wanted to visit the shrine—it meant a lot to them.

The residents wanted peace and quiet—it meant a lot

to them.

It meant a lot to the council, who wanted money, and the hoteliers and the licensed schlock souvenir pedlars.

Rome applied for planning permission to build a Basilica in the Garden to replace the tatty cardboard icon for the veneration of Our Lady of Cheltenhamshire.

The tenacious journalist also discovered reports of a strange light that had appeared in the early morning sky over GCHQ on the day of the visitation that the authorities dismissed casually as meteorite activity.

That very same meteorite evening, a woman smelling of peppermint and roses sat down in the front row of an auditorium to watch Seaweed & Troy as a guest of honour, relieved to have got out and met some real people.

# THE MACHINE OF HAPPINESS (I)

I know what you're thinking—how do I get my hands on that machine of happiness? How much does it cost? Are there concessions? Can I pay in interest free instalments? Everyone is searching for the machine of happiness and Bob Brady had one in his flat. Bob had invented the first contraption for producing happiness. Everyone was going to want a slice of that happiness action. Bob was going to rent out the machine and punters were going to pay handsomely for it.

All you had to do was put your head inside the machine of happiness. It wanted your fears and sadness. Imagine your fear is clay and the machine is the potter, and the potter is going to put hands of such gentle kindness onto your fear and your fear is going to dissolve and the light of yourself is going to return home to you. Imagine that! Sign me up! That's what you're thinking!

That crazy son of a bitch had invented the first working machine of happiness.

It stood happily in the corner of his small flat waiting to make people happy.

Alleluia.

# THE CARETAKER

Joseph Hawthorne was literally a blast from the past. The past being the 1920s! He would be right at home in a P.G. Wodehouse novel. He spoke with a cut-glass accent widely heard on the BBC in the first half of the 20th century. This made him socially distinctive in the 21st century. He was tall, slender and respectably bespectacled. Casual dress meant wearing a pinstripe suit and cravat. He felt comfortable and relaxed in formal wear. Hawthorne had never worn or owned a tracksuit. He'd never washed dishes, hoovered up, and certainly never cooked a meal in his life. His beloved nanny was now his children's nanny.

Hawthorne attended Eton College before receiving a first-class honours degree in the classics from Cambridge University where he was a talented member of the Cambridge University Footlights Dramatic Club. He went on to carve out a highly successful career as a leading psychiatrist; he was far too discreet and modest to ever reveal the fact that his clients ranged from royalty to prime ministers and A-list celebrities. Joseph's inherited noble blood and aristocratic mannerisms came from his mother—The Lady Mabel Hawthorne. Her father and Joe's grandfather was the Earl of Cheltenhamshire. Joe's father, an untitled wealthy self-made businessman, met the young Lady Mabel Carrington at a Cotswold Life Magazine charity ball.

Hawthorne would roll up to training every day in his 4-door saloon. It just happened to be a 1925 Rolls Royce

New Phantom 4-door saloon; commendably, he was driving in place of where a chauffeur would have customarily sat. In the comfortable passenger seats, normally reserved for aristocratic family members of a period drama, a large net full of footballs, bibs and cones sat. Many times Hawthorne would use the stately Roller to taxi injured players to accident and emergency before returning them to their homes in plaster cast style.

If it were muddy underfoot he would remove his classic black brogue shoes to reveal his sock garters reassuringly keeping his socks up before putting on his Le Chameau Wellington Boots whilst sat on the Roller's grand door-cill footstep. If it were raining he would enlist one of the younger academy boys to hold his black city umbrella whilst he gave out instructions. He would make notes in a black moleskine notebook using a fountain pen that once belonged to W.H. Auden. The team sheet was a calligraphic work of art that when pinned to the notice board looked similar to a royal proclamation nailed to a broad oak tree.

Hawthorne was unfailingly polite; he rarely swore but when he did it was extremely hard not to burst out laughing at the incongruity. His half-time team talks were the stuff of legend. One first half performance saw his side hit the goalposts on four different occasions and the crossbar on three, which must have been some sort of record, whilst the opposition had just three shots on goal, all of which found the back of the net. Losing 3:0 they were in serious danger of losing their season's unbeaten record. The scene was set for some Hawthorne oratory. As the young players sat down in the dressing room they looked to their manager for inspiration, who was calmly stood in the centre of the changing room.

"Gentlemen, we seem to have got ourselves into a bit of a bind. I have received a letter here from a Mr G Post and a Mr C Bar that I would like to read to you.

'To whom it may concern,

'Would you all jolly well just fuck-orf please and stop hitting us, as it's getting exceedingly tedious and boring. May we make a polite suggestion that you recalibrate your heads and feet by five inches?

'Thanking you in advance, Goalpost & Crossbar.'"

It did the trick—the Academy fought back to draw the match: 3:3.

Twice, the beautiful game was nearly lost to him: the first time when a new academy player broke his jaw for substituting him and for good measure fractured a couple of ribs with well-aimed kicks, causing a lung to collapse and leaving him gasping for air. He understood the adolescent anger: he felt the fists of his abusive father on that young man; it was like being beaten twice. *The world is full of so much stuff leaking out of people: that so little is ever fixed or set free is its greatest sadness, its greatest challenge,* he said to his wife.

The second time was last summer when the most gifted player he had ever worked with died of leukaemia. During the many hospital visits, he witnessed a vital athletic teenager turn to fragile skin and bones.

Dressed in the club's kit, complete with boots, shin-pads and goalkeeping gloves, the boys carried his coffin into the church. Joe wrote and read the elegy; he put that young man back together, bone by balletic bone, pass by slide rule pass, tackle by tackle, goal by goal, before finally blowing a long last farewell into his whistle.

Joe's passion for football was born at the age of eight when his father took him to watch his first non-league match at Whaddon Road. It was a midweek evening kick-off in November, which added to its sense of way-past-bedtime adventure. He'd never seen so many people in one place in his life. The turnstiles were like the entrance to a magical world with the pitch at the heart of the kingdom, illuminated by its own floodlit suns. Fans were chanting songs and clapping while the players warmed up, music and announcements blared out of the tinny tannoy system and the winter's night air held it all a little longer for your ears to enjoy. It was a feast for his young senses: the vivid colour of hats and scarves, cigarette smoke perfuming the air mingled with the smell of hot dogs, Bovril and burgers. The atmosphere produced a wonderful, crude, life-affirming sense of humour from characters of Falstaffian proportions. He laughed so much that he nearly wet himself. The away team had come all the way from an exotic place called Corby Town to visit the magical kingdom. Joe was hooked; he would give anything to run out onto the playing field, his name printed in the match programme. The names of the players would become immortalised heroes, which even now, forty years later, he could remember fondly.

Sadly for Joe, he was not ordained with an ounce of natural footballing ability—while some sportsmen squeeze every drop of talent they have out of themselves to make the grade, no amount of mechanical squeezing of Joe's ability would produce a single drop of the much-dreamed-of elixir.

The same year he watched his first match, his mother died suddenly. Now a father with two boys of nine and ten, he often thought of the love his mother must have given him that he never truly remembered. *Where does all that love go if you can't remember it? Is it worthless? Wasted?* He thought of all the love he had poured into his children and whether if he died today they would remember any of it. He knew that his mother's love had sunk into him. He often wondered from a professional viewpoint if it had anything to do with him being the way he was?

His work at the academy began with some voluntary sports psychology sessions, but his talents quickly led to him taking his coaching badges before becoming the highly successful, nationally recognised academy coach. The players worshipped the grass and whitewash he walked on. Hawthorne was a cerebral coach; all his players understood their roles within the team and they were teak-tough mentally and physically. The players would run their hearts out to bursting for him. They knew how much he cared—not just about winning, but about them personally—they trusted him. While his team was modern and innovative in their tactics and conditioning, they were a throwback to a forgotten age when it came to behaviour. He put into reverse all they had learnt in the past from former coaches and television. Hawthorne coached the futility of badmouthing the officials, of ruing bad luck and of the beauty of sportsmanship. They learnt the power of understanding their own emotions and others; when, as young men, they fell off the Hawthorne wagon of personal development, he was there to put an arm around them.

His influence didn't end at the training ground; he organised trips to the Royal Shakespeare Theatre in Stratford-Upon-Avon, he gave them copies of his favourite passages and quotes from novels, television, radio and poetry to read and movies to watch for 'homework'—small nuggets of wisdom—all paid out of his own pocket. For those who couldn't read, he set aside his own time to help teach them. The players loved to listen to Hawthorne's recitals and impressions and were always putting in requests for performances in breaks between sessions, which, after some coyness, Hawthorne loved to oblige. His repertoire was broad, from the classic speeches of Shakespeare, Churchill, JFK, Mandela, Lincoln and King to lines from Jack Nicholson and Russell Crowe. On Remembrance Day he would recite a poem to them; last year it was *The Christmas Truce* by Carol Ann Duffy—'and make of a battleground a football pitch'—before observing with them a 2-minute silence.

When the time came to tell so many of them that they weren't going to make the grade as a professional, Joe always told them himself, face to face. When he saw their gratitude for what he had done for them rise up courageously through the shattering sadness to thank him, it brought a lump of pride to his throat.

Despite his intellectual, calm approach, nobody ever underestimated Hawthorne's determination and will to win. If that will to win ever escaped from the prison of his body, it would be like Godzilla smashing every opposition side from the face of the Earth.

For the last time, Hawthorne called over the academy squad. "Did you all watch *Full Metal Jacket* last night? Good." He then proceeded flawlessly to imitate Gunnery Sergeant Hartman:

"I am Academy Manager Hawthorne, your senior instructor. From now on you will speak only when spoken to, and the first and last words out of your mouths will be

'Sir'. Do you maggots understand?"

Team: "Sir, yes sir."

"Bullshit, I can't hear you!"

"SIR, YES SIR!"

"What's your position, boy?"

"Striker, sir."

"Show me your goal-scoring celebration!"

"Sir, yes sir!"

"You need more funk in that funky chicken next time. What's your position, boy?"

"Goalkeeper, sir."

"All goalkeepers are crazy."

"Sir, yes sir!"

"Show me how crazy you are, golo!"

"Sir, yes sir!"

Golo proclaims himself to be a human hedge-strimmer and strims the heads of his teammates with his hand, making a buzzing sound.

"You're a credit to your team and goalkeepers, boy. What's your name, soldier?"

"Andrew Bassett, sir."

"That a dog's name?"

"Different spelling, sir, only one 't' in basset hound, sir."

"An educated dog, I like that! Make like a hound!"

"Sir, yes sir!"

On all fours, Andy 'Bass' Bassett engaged in an impressive hound impersonation: sniffing, scratching, panting and howling before returning to Hawthorne's side and cocking his leg as if pissing on his shoes. With much merriment Hawthorne went through the whole academy team one by one; not a player was left unturned.

On Saturday afternoon, after forty years of wringing out his talent, Hawthorne would proudly step out as the manager of his boyhood club, with his name printed in the match day programme.

# JESUS

Robert 'Sitting Bull' Brady had always wanted to be a writer. His sanity was a major impediment to him achieving that dream, along with the hemispheres of his brain being perfectly formed to make him a computer programming genius. Before taking early retirement Bob spent his entire working life at a well-known local aerospace instruments manufacturer where he let his brain do the talking, hidden away in a small room not much bigger than a broom cupboard. When the big cheeses from America visited, Bob's bosses kept him hidden away due to his dishevelled appearance and the whiff of cider and onions from his daily ploughman's lunchtime pub routine. The Yanks weren't stupid. The suits quickly demonstrated they didn't know what the hell they were talking about. "Where's the guy that programmed this?" they asked. So they sent for 'Jesus' as he was known from the cupboard. Jesus would appear Christ-like: the living embodiment of the Shroud of Turin, wearing sandals and twiddling his moustache, behaving perfectly like himself, no artifice—just authentically eccentric and talented. The Yanks instantly loved him. When Jesus spoke they listened and nodded and got excited and became his disciples; from then on they would always say 'bring us Jesus' and flew him out to the States on regular visits.

Jesus helped keep planes flying like the Concorde and the Yanks paid him handsomely, which meant he could attend more beer festivals and extend his lunchtime visits to the pub.

Bob never married. He did fall in love once on a trip to visit his brother in South Wales. He fell in love with a woman who was taking the money at the Severn Bridge crossing toll booth.

"Good morning, how much is it to see the Welsh Trolls that live under the bridge?" Bob said good humouredly, handing over a ten-pound note.

"It's all included in the price," said the attendant, smiling cheerfully and returning him his change and a receipt.

"Thank you," Bob said.

"Remember to keep your windows up," the woman said.

That was the brief encounter that besotted Bob. He knew by the time the barrier went up to send him on his merry way she was the girl he wanted to spend the rest of his life with. Bob immediately got off at the next junction, turned around, crossed back over the bridge, exited the next junction, crossed back over the bridge again and returned to the same toll barrier. Nothing was going to get in the way of his love for this woman. The second brief meeting just confirmed what his heart already knew. The woman didn't recognise him—she saw a lot of men during the course of her shift. The third time, he bought her some flowers from the service station and handed them over to her in the booth.

"Never let there be barriers between us," he said, smiling flirtatiously. She'd never been given gifts before whilst at work. Infatuation didn't stop its journey there. Expensive chocolates, then champagne, followed with a handwritten card with his telephone number. It was costing him a small fortune but he was crazy about her. You can't put a price tag on love. He never got to see his brother. What Bob couldn't see from his car was that the woman was heavily pregnant with her second child and this was her last day at work. She didn't call security or do anything to discourage the advances of Bob—after all why should she? It was like Santa Claus arriving on his sled every 25 minutes with a wedding list gift! She would tell her husband they were leaving presents. The bloodsucking woman never got to receive the expensive perfume Bob had bought her. By that time, her shift had finished, and she was on her way home loaded up to the gunnels with the strange admirer's gifts. Bob's heart sank when a middle-aged man with a beard appeared at the booth of his great love.

She never called. Over the coming months he made a lot of unsuccessful trips to see his brother. With hope in his heart he paid to line up at every booth checking to see if he could find her. Night and day he tried—it was agonising. His love grew stronger. The thought of another man touching her made him sick. He purchased a diamond ring that he kept in the glove compartment, ready for the day he found her again. He wasn't going to let her get away a second time. Eventually the whole episode took a terrible toll on Bob, literally. Broken hearted, Bob gave up. He would love her until the day he died. Bob never married.

He never wrote a novel either. Bob pursued his literary dream with the same zealous fervour he poured into the Lady of the Severn. He craved artistic perfection. He wanted to write a fiction supreme, an expression of words so powerful and eloquent that it would change the world.

The words never gave up this secret to Bob. They never lied down on the page with the equation solved, the code broken. His imagination skilfully avoided originality. Bob entered every literature competition and contest imaginable in the firm belief winning was a foregone conclusion. In disbelief Bob would re-read again and again the winning entries, checking they had not missed his name off the list. Bob even contacted the administrators to confirm they had omitted him by error. "I'm sorry, sir," they would say, "there is definitely no mistake, the competition was very fierce this year."

The constant rejection began to quickly eat away at Bob's soul. Failure turned to jealousy, jealousy to hatred. A string of judges and their families received anonymous death threats. Finally, in desperation, Bob turned to the vultures circling his misery—vanity publishers. They gratefully took his money and put him in print. The shame ripped through Bob as if he'd paid for an escort. Realising he'd made a terrible mistake, he tried to liberate his trapped poems and stories from vanity's guilty brothel. The ISBN number on the 'collection' was little more than a prisoner's serial number. Not even a pardon from the queen could secure their freedom now. Increasingly deluded he tried unsuccessfully to pay a ransom to the publisher to remove his work. Bob believed his incarcerated work of art was a winning breakthrough masterpiece—if only it could break out. It was no good; it was now 'previously published', it was dead.

Bob was on a slippery literary slope. If there was a sanatorium for the unpublished Bob was dangerously close to admission.

Desperate and depraved he stole the words of others—

dead or alive. For the first time, he knew what it felt like to be a success, to see his name long listed, shortlisted and to gloriously win prizes and to call himself a writer.

It didn't last long; the envy and suspicion of losing contestants is most efficient when it comes to dobbing in cheats. Bob was quickly and ignominiously stripped of his awards, given a lifetime ban, stoned half to death by wordsmiths' unforgiving words. Bob put down his pen.

# BURNING RHYME

Fortunately, for Bob Brady's literary dream and broken heart, luck was at hand in the wacky onset of his madness. The madness mended his heart. It also acted like a benevolent creative worm boring into previously inaccessible seams of writing gold. Suddenly, the windmills of his mind were filled with the creative breath of Hermes. Chapter after chapter, verse after verse, act after act flowed from the originality of his new-minted mind. Plays, poetry and novels graced the floor of his study just waiting for the world undiscovered. A literary agent would swallow dive naked with excitement into them. Later, scholars would refer to these magnificent works of literature as the Wellington Square Manuscripts.

Bob's nighttime life was now largely dedicated to his literary pursuits. He rarely slept more than a few hours. At 1 in the morning he was sat up in bed staring at his electric toothbrush sat on the floor in its charging mount flashing with a comforting green light. He thought it looked like an upside down lighthouse warning him not to trip on the rocky edge of the rug. These are the thoughts you can expect inside the mind of a madman. Guided by the lighthouse, he got out of bed and walked over to his window. Naked and unseen he watched suspiciously the brand new pay and display parking metres wearing their black uniforms with their trusty lieutenant signs nearby. To Bob they were like the council's private paramilitary soldiers. They even had their own serial numbers. Bob was biding his time. As soon as he'd perfected his levitation powers he would rip them from the ground, sending them crashing through the windows of the Highways & Parking Department offices like deadly missiles. By the time Bob had finished they would need a Star Wars defence system to protect them from incoming parking meters and signs. Pay and display machines would lie dying on the council floors, their guts ripped open, spilling coined blood.

Bob was in the mood for poetry. He would summon the Great Spirit for inspiration, sacrificing some of his best-loved words from his favourite poet Federico Garcia Lorca—the great Spanish poet who was so tragically executed by another fascist regime's firing squad during the Spanish Civil War. He lovingly wrote down the lines onto small pieces of scrap paper. It felt good to do this, gave him a sense of a beautiful power, a beautiful power he now possessed. Bob filled his peace pipe with marijuana and began smoking; he lit each piece of paper from his pipe before placing them in an ashtray to burn, offering the verse up to the Great Spirit whilst chanting between puffs:

"Wey ha da heya na

"'A wild crowd of young breezes over the river.'

"Wey ha da heya na

"'In the sunbaked path, I've seen the good lizard (drop of crocodile).'

"Heya ha no da

"'His voice had something of sea without light, and orange squeezed dry.'

"Wey ha da heya na

"'Castanet. Castanet. Castanet. Sonorous scarab.'

"Ah hey yo ha da hey

"'At five in the afternoon. It was exactly five in the afternoon.'

"Wey ha da heya na

"'The round silence of night, one note on the stave of the infinite.'

"Ah hey yo ha da hey

"'A single bird is singing. The air is cloning it.'

"Wey ha da heya na."

Bob's chanting fell silent as he slipped into a happy dream like state of paralysis; a vision came to him that he would soon be writing into a fully formed mini play.

# WHADDNEY THE ROBIN (I)

Whaddney the Robin left the nest of his flat in Wellington Square in the full glorious bliss of ignorance for the short walk to the football club. Melodiously, he sang a happy fluting whistle into the amnesia afternoon, waving cheerfully to the assembled birdwatchers. Robins are sociable creatures. For thirty happy years Whaddney had made this short flight. He was in his prime as a mascot.

It was not the innocent sparrow with his bow and arrow that killed Whaddney Robin; it was a Colombian Condor. In the midst of the hasty preparation for the match, the 'services are no longer required' letter was still in the chairman's out-tray. At just 5 feet 2 inches, Whaddney's diminutive stature no longer met the new job description. The man who did was a recently retired police officer standing at 6 feet 4 inches. This was a big gig for the Condor. At just fifty years old and with a sizeable pension, this was a dream start to his new career. A lot of masonic arm-twisting of the chairman had gone on to land this part. Getting a mascot job is literally dead mascot's shoes—it's a dream fan job that gets under your costume skin and stays there forever. The investiture of a new club mascot is like a coronation. You rarely see these jobs advertised; the number of applicants would be overwhelming.

The average age of a mascot is seventy—it is literally a job for life. It wouldn't be long before bears, wombles, eels, tigers and other assorted mascots would be keeling over on the football stage. When the paramedics removed their headgear, they would be shocked at the toll a mascot's life had taken; petrified mummies were better preserved. Eventually the Football Association would act to establish a sanctuary for retired mascots, similar to a donkey sanctuary.

The Condor was taking a great risk with his life. He loathed football with a passion; everything about football made him sick. He was an undercover mascot, driven by the desire for a different vocation. If the truth were discovered, he would be captured and footballed to death— buried up to his neck on the pitch while footballs were kicked at his head by masked mascots until he expired. It was a risk worth taking, for this was the chance of a lifetime for the Condor to showcase his acting skills. He would be the main attraction, stealing the limelight from those professional pufta players; fans would be buying season tickets just to see him as if he were Gielgud playing Hamlet. It was a stepping-stone to BAFTAs and Oscars.

When the Condor saw Whaddney arriving on his new manor, he did what birds do instinctively to defend their territory—he ambushed him in the toilets and kicked the shit out of him. While Whaddney threw himself bravely and pugnaciously at the Condor, he was no match for a retired police officer who over the years had honed thuggery to a fine art form. Dishing out a beating to the innocent brought back happy memories for him—it was like the good old days.

Beaten and bowed, Whaddney staggered away from the ground like a sick mascot on the way to the mascot graveyard via the pub.

# BURNING RHYME

**by Robert Brady (taken from the Wellington Square Manuscripts)**

A dramaticule

for Federico Garcia Lorca

CAST:
Federico Garcia Lorca
Jesus
Poetic Voice
Soldier's Voice

## <u>CURTAIN</u>

Stage in darkness. The audience have listened to Wayward Bob's previous poetic sacrifices and chanting.

An invisible stagehand cranks a large full moon into position above the stage, bathing it in moonlight. The light reveals a middle-aged man dressed in a white linen shirt, beige summer chinos and wearing sandals. He looks like Jesus and is stood at a full-length mirror; he sprays himself liberally about the neck with cologne, the spray's mist visible in the light. On the floor, an ashtray is full of burnt pieces of paper.

The theatre fills with the smell of mint and orange.

To the centre rear of the stage a spotlight reveals the handsome Lorca in his late thirties standing with his hands at his side perfectly still; his large forehead pale as the moon, the cloudy sky into which his dark winged eyebrows want to take flight. He is wearing a black tuxedo with a dicky bow and short-heeled black leather flamenco dance shoes. His thick brylcreemed hair is as sleek as a black Spanish bull's hide. With a ramrod straight back and proud chest he stares out at the audience.

A flamenco guitar breaks the silence with a loud rasgueado rolling like Andalucian thunder before stopping suddenly.

Lorca takes five long, elegant, proud steps forward with the movement and perfect posture of a flamenco dancer, his elbows always leading the way accompanied by the distinctive inward and outward use of the hands.

Unseen, a guitarist begins playing a Faruca with slow rhythmical chords. Lorca turns and travels sideways across the stage with a series of slow balletic pirouettes, rising on the toes of his feet, keeping his heels off the stage—the guitarist accompanies him, following his tempo. You can hear the shuffle and swish of the shoes in the theatre, the last sequence of rotations are faster, accompanied by kneeling spins before sliding elegantly on bent knee into a lunge pose. As he stops, he loudly snaps his fingers, holding the position; the guitarist stops playing.

POETIC VOICE: The afternoon says: 'I'm thirsty for

shadow!' And the moon: 'I want stars.' The crystal fountain asks for lips, the wind for sighs.

The guitarist continues playing; Lorca travels back across the stage, improvising the glides and pirouettes. Subtle differences mark each dance movement, always ending with the snap of his fingers in various poses, always beautiful, always dancing on the sole of his shoes.

POETIC VOICE: The air, pregnant with rainbows, shatters its mirrors over the grove.
(dance—snap of the fingers)
POETIC VOICE: The keel of the moon rips purple clouds.
(dance—snap of the fingers)
POETIC VOICE: In the spider of the hand, you crimp the warm air.
(dance—snap of the fingers)
POETIC VOICE: The moon, nearly smothered with flowers & with branches, fights them off with moonbeams, like an octopus in silver.
(dance—snap of the fingers)
POETIC VOICE: Over the yellow wind, the bell notes flower.
(dance—snap of the fingers
POETIC VOICE: The backwater of your mouth, under our thickening kisses.

Lorca pirouettes towards the centre front of the stage before walking to a stop and standing still, feet together, hands by his side, staring out at the audience.

POETIC VOICE: Then I realised I had been murdered. They

looked for me in cafes, in cemeteries, in churches, but they didn't find me. They never found me? No. They never found me.

SOLDIER'S VOICE: I gave that fat-head a shot in the head.

POETIC VOICE: The song I'll never speak, on the tip of my tongue fell asleep.

SOLDIER'S VOICE: I fired two bullets into his ass for being a queer.

Lorca strips off his jacket, shirt and dicky bow, throwing them into the wings to reveal his torso before shouting a loud dramatic cry in Spanish and accompanying it with the stomping of his feet, the first use of the clack of his heels, signalling the beginning of a charismatic and virtuoso zapeateo footwork section. The dance begins slowly before gaining in dazzling power and tempo, a short strutting, snorting rest then follows each crescendo before starting the cycle again, travelling across the entire stage.

He is accompanied by percussive hand clapping, flamenco guitar and Spanish shouts of encouragement, all unseen. The dance builds to an emotional finale of dance and sound, it ends with a loud Whitmanesque yawp, a life shouting for life. Lorca kneels at the front centre of the stage, facing the wings, breathing heavily, sweat running down his chest, his hands behind his back as if facing a firing squad.

Jesus walks across the stage and circles Lorca twice before kneeling directly opposite Lorca in the same position, the two men now face to face.

LORCA: You summoned me?

JESUS: I was burning your poems for inspiration.

LORCA (smiling): They felt no pain.

JESUS: Were you scared at the end?

LORCA: I had never been so pregnant with ripe poems, I could feel them shaking with fear inside me; I held them like a father—we died together.

Lorca leans towards Jesus. Like a swan, his nose slowly glides up and then down the length of Jesus's neck without touching it, breathing in deeply the perfume of mint and orange. Jesus could feel the warm air from his nostrils and mouth on his skin.

LORCA: You smell of the homeland I loved.

(Lorca pauses)

Did they find my body?

JESUS: No.

LORCA: Good.

JESUS: Why is that good?

LORCA: You cannot cradle and rock with guilty grief a country of bones in your arms, all warmth and flesh long since gone. Spain must always be lost, unable to mourn, to forget, to never be free of the pain of killing itself. Let them look for me forever! This is my last will and testament.

JESUS: I would rock you with love. I have never felt the desire to kiss a man before.

LORCA: Why do you want to kiss me?

JESUS: I want to kiss you for your words, to thank you for your heart.

LORCA: My words and heart would like that.

Jesus leans forward with his eyes closed and places his mouth tenderly against the mouth of Federico Garcia Lorca, kissing him amongst the moonbeams with the most delicate kiss of his life.

The stage fades to darkness.
POETIC VOICE: The sun carries of your soul to make it into light.

# <u>CURTAIN</u>

# NATIONAL GIVE UP PORNOGRAPHY DAY

The sun had risen on National Give Up Pornography Day, pouring through the windows of Wellington Square like a knickerless nurse flashing her yellow pussy. Earth's bow wave pushed on deep through the open legs of space, the dark petals of her vagina unfolding around its head. Gravity's leash pulled us all into its dark boudoir.

That mid-October morning the lime leaves were sniffing the warm morning air trembling with orgasm. It was without a trace of autumn; it had forgotten what month it was. It was a thermostatically perfect bonus summer's day in October. The fallen dying lime leaves opened their eyes, wanting to fly back to the orgy tree; they couldn't believe their bad luck.

The retreating summer had cashed in all its nectar points, turned out its warm pockets and bribed the entire day from autumn. It was giddy with a cheating death row reprieve. *Just one day mind you*, said autumn, stashing the cash in her stockings.

Citizens were stepping out into the amnesia of a day that had lost its way. The saucy summer nurse was bathing them all in golden sunlight, sticking a bonus badge on their chests, which they were wearing with gratitude. The apple tree was heavy with drooping fruit, braless. The day could have won a beauty contest.

It was a beautiful day to give up pornography.

# MOOM MONSTERS (III)

A beefy man with a big chest, a lot of puff, good eyesight, and a belly like granddad's had the great honour of being stationed in a tall watchtower with lots of cider and thick sandwiches to keep his belly company. He was watching the sea for the tell-tale signs of the Moom approaching. It was like being in the crow's nest of one of Christopher Columbus's ships during the Age of Discovery; imagine the excitement of being the first European to set eyes on a new land or island? The watchman would not be shouting land ahoy but Moom ahoy!

The Moom watchman was a veteran of Moom festivals but his wonderment at their arrival was still childlike. He was as excited as you are, Freddie, on Christmas Eve! Nobody knew where the Moom lived for eight months of the year. It was a mystery. A mystery we will discover in later times of bed, along with many other splendid adventures!

Far out to sea the watchman caught sight of what he was watching for. The sea was standing up as tall as the Eiffel Tower in a gigantic churning, bubbling tsunami bow wave. Now you know why the harbour walls had to be so well constructed. He took a large swig of his cider and a deep breath before putting a rare shell trumpet made from the shell of the Great Sea Snail to his cidery lips. The trumpet was beautifully engraved with elaborate patterns and mounted on the watchtower like a cannon defending a port from invaders. The marvellous, unmistakable, deep, vibrating, droning sound of the trumpet filled the air, as if the roaring sea was speaking to the Mu. The people cheered wildly, parents picked up their children to savour the moment and kissed them with joyful smacking kisses as fireworks celebrated, crackling in the sky. I know it's a bit yucky but for centuries tradition had demanded that upon hearing the sound of the shell trumpet the girls kissed the boys and the boys kissed the girls. If there was somebody you liked in school—let's say Connie Salt from 7E who you keep talking about—ok, ok, I won't mention her again—anyway, you needed to make sure you were strategically standing very close to whoever it was you may or may not like, otherwise your rival would steal your heart's desire! The sound of the shell trumpet was like musical mistletoe. 'The Moom are coming! The Moom are coming!'

The Mu also knew the Moom by two other less used names: The Roly Poly and the Wily-Wily for reasons that will become clear with some explaining.

As the Moom Monsters came closer, the Mu could see the glowing hulls of their bellies illuminating the sea and the sky like giant lanterns of floating golden light. This year was a very special year. In the middle of the Moomeration—for that was the name given to the spectacle unfolding before their eyes—in the middle of the family of Mooms was a baby Moom! Mind you, Freddie, we need to keep a sense of perspective on the size of a baby Moom. It didn't weight 6 pounds 4 ounces like you did when you were born! A baby Moom weighed at least 20 tonnes—three times that of a grown elephant! Just being smaller wasn't the only dead giveaway that this was a baby: a baby Moom does not have a glowing golden light in their belly. He—for the baby was a boy—would have to wait another 50 years before he acquired this magical phenomenon. Baby Mooms on average appeared once every hundred years! They lived to a very ripe age. Nobody knew how old the Moom lived for because nobody had out survived a Moom!

For many of the Mu this would have been the first time they'd seen a baby. It just added to the excitement. 'A baby Moom! Look! A baby Moom!' Everybody loved a newborn baby. Things were about to get even more exciting.

As they approached the shallow shore they began to curl themselves up into balls, otherwise they would get beached on the bottom due to their great size. They looked like giant cannon or ten pin bowling balls. Centuries of Moom arrivals had carved out a smooth pothole-free Moom motorway leading from the shore to the plateau of the high hills. It would have made a great downhill ski slope. They rolled in single file up the ski slope; the baby Moom was given a gentle nudge by his parents to help him roly-poly up the steepest part of the slope to his new home and the comfortable bedding prepared by the Mu. So now you can see why some of the Mu called the Moom Monsters the Roly Poly. In all, 21 Mooms were checked in to their hillside hotel with panoramic sea views over the City of Murria. All were present and correct plus one.

# HALF-TIME TEAM TALK

"What did the manager say to you at half time?" asked the gathered media.

"It's a long story," replied the Condors' skipper.

The story began with the Condors' goalkeeper being greeted enthusiastically for the first time by the home fans behind the goal all wearing their blue, red and green sombreros with pride. The gringo army were in full swing—maracas beat out—shush shush shushshushshush shushshushshushshush CONDORS!

Despite an early Colombian wave of optimism and the best first-half performance of the season, the Condors found themselves trudging down the tunnel losing 2:0— both goals conceded to cruel deflections. Deflections were on a hattrick! Despite being battered, the away team had Deflector of the Rovers on their side and he was unplayable. No amount of training and practice can prevent a deflected goal; it will punish the brave players courageously trying to block a shot equally as much as the chicken-hearted turning their backs on the ball. In this instance, the brave were punished.

To make matters worse, the talisman (or in this case talisbird) mascot of good luck had got into a right rumpus. It started when the jubilant away supporters with typical fan ingenuity started humorously mocking the home fans:

"You woke up this morning and your Robin was gone

"Ooh wee chirpy chirpy cheep cheep

"Chirpy chirpy cheep cheep chirp

"Where's your Robin gone

"Where's your Robin gone..."

Not content with taunting the home crowd, they turned their creative attention towards the Cotswold Condor whose annoying touch line over acting and attention seeking had drawn unnecessary notice to himself; pointing in his direction, they sang:

"All the birds of the air fell a sighing and a sobbing

"When they heard of the death of poor Cock Robin

"When they heard of the death of poor Cock Robin!"

They accompanied the old English folksong by flapping their arms like wings and rubbing imaginary tears from their eyes with the sides of their fists. The Cotswold Condors' mascot inexperience, combined with his first match stage nerves and hatred of football fans quickly got the better of him.

The Cotswold Condor started making his own inciting graphic gesticulations to the away supporters and in doing so was in breach of his contractual obligations, not to mention the mascot code of conduct. The police, fearing the Condor's action would cause trouble, sensibly tried to calm him down but this just added to his humiliation. The Condor went into a flying rage, resisting arrest very effectively by wind milling wild haymakers at his former colleagues. Quickly realising they were getting the worse of the argument, a police officer drew her Taser and shouted, "Taser! Taser!" A red dot appeared on the torso of the Condor. "I'm going to Taser you now!" said the police officer calmly and she did, much to the relief of her colleagues. Two copper wire probes sprung out, hitting the Condor just beneath his right wing. The shock temporarily suspended his central Condor nervous system, incapacitating him enough for four police officers to wing cuff him and carry him off to the bird meat wagon, much to the unbridled joy of the away supporters and the embarrassment of the home. As the half-time whistle sounded, the Condors were Condorless—a bad omen.

The Cheltenhamshire fans were in desperate need of some comfort food and queued patiently for the 'Bogotá Burger' with some strange-looking black fried 'Colombian Onions'. The sombreros became lids for depression.

While the assistant manager ensured the players took on some fluids and dispensed some perfunctory cheery optimism, Hawthorne had locked himself in the toilet. No, he hadn't lost his bottle; on the contrary, he was about to make one of the bravest decisions ever made in the history of football. His pinstripe suit was now in its travel bag hanging on the back of the toilet door. He sat on the toilet seat, now wearing a one-piece beige cotton dress with long lace sleeves and a navy-blue doll collar; his wife had bought it for him for Father's Day. Nerves meant that he had trouble zipping it up at the back. Joe covered his neck with a silk scarf and wore black leggings with trainers on his feet. His phone pinged with a text—*running late, but looking great!—Stephen—Smiley Face*. Hawthorne quickly texted back—*I'm in the toilet—petrified—Joe—Face Screaming in Fear*. He opened a small compact, competently applying black mascara and eyeliner before spraying two puffs of elegant Diorella by Christian Dior on either side of his neck. He felt a maternal love from the memory of the scent and the ladies clothing, like being swaddled in a towel.

"Where's the 'gaffa'?" said Dangerous Dave Dangerfield, the burly centre back and skipper.

"He's in the toilet!" said Stephen Fry, breezing into the changing rooms. Fry is an ardent Norwich City fan (the Canaries). "Bloody bad luck, fellas, you played them off the park in that half, make sure you switch on your deflector shields to full blast for the second!" Fry banged on the one locked toilet door, "Come on Joe—it's time to come out!" Hawthorne took a deep breath before rising to unbolt the door.

"Thanks for coming, Stephen," said Hawthorne, embracing his friend and sometime patient.

"I wouldn't miss it for the world, darling, I was in town anyway." Fry took Hawthorne by the hand as if accepting a dance, walking him proudly into the centre of the changing room. "Doesn't he look magnificent?" said Fry, smiling proudly.

"What's up, haven't you seen a man dressed as a woman before?" said Joe in response to the incredulous stares and open mouths that were too dumbstruck to even form an ironic wolf whistle.

"No, never," said 'Gary 'Gibbo' Gibbons the left back, not realising it wasn't a rhetorical question.

"Please, sit down, gentlemen, and listen up," said Hawthorne, surprising himself with his own confidence. "This is part of who I really am: a husband, a father, a football manager, and a man who feels safe and happy when he dresses like a woman." He paused as he sat on an unexpected swell of emotion rising inside of him as he pictured his mother.

"Is it a kinky sex thing?" asked Gibbo, still fascinated.

"I am going out there, back to the dugout, as the first cross-dressing football league manager. Together we are going to create history—you are going to make me the first winning football league cross-dressing manager."

"I'm gay—I've always been gay!" said 'Robo' Robinson, the creative centre midfield dynamo, standing up defiantly and taking his place alongside Fry and Hawthorne.

"Bravo, young man!" said Fry, patting him on the back. "Anyone else?"

The players looked around furtively, greeting each other with frowned shakes of the head. The referee knocked on the door and entered the changing room.

"Two min...utes," he said, staring at Fry and Hawthorne standing in his dress.

"Thank you, sir," said Hawthorne politely.

"Don't do it boss, they'll eat you alive!" exclaimed Mummford.

Hawthorne circled the room, holding eye contact with all of his players before commencing his oratory:

"Let us stand in this life, on this ground, on this pitch, as who we truly are. Sons of Cheltenhamshire, my brothers! I see in your eyes the same fear that would take the heart of me, when we forsake our friends and break all bonds of fellowship. But it is not this day.

"Ninety minutes of shattered confidence and fear when another record-breaking defeat comes crashing down! But it is not this day! This day we fight! By all that you hold dear on this good earth, I bid you stand, Men of the West!"

"Come on!" shouted Dangerous, fired up, clapping his hands. "We can do it!"

The team rose as one with the sound of well-motivated studs pawing the floor for action. "That's the spirit, Canaries!" said Fry. As the players purposefully left the changing room for the second half they all high-fived

Hawthorne and Fry. Robo was the last to leave, slipping under Hawthorne's outstretched hand and hugging his waist. A nearby volunteer St John Ambulance worker swore he heard Mummford shouting, "Let's save the hobbits!" as he ran out onto the pitch.

# SHAMBLES

Gittler had completely lost his grip on the situation; the Garden was a glorious shambles. Powerless, he was like a fish out of water, or in his case a dictator out of tarmac. Dusky's shyness had become embarrassing; people were impatiently beginning to question whether Gittler was just an attention seeking fraud. The stress of it all had begun to weigh heavily on him. It was as if he'd personally promised them a Glastonbury headline superstar act and the fans were getting restless waiting for the performance to start. He was desperate for Dusky to walk out on stage.

There were now at least two thousand souls in the Garden, including regional news media—a record attendance. A canary yellow, avian humanoid, dressed as Big Bird from Sesame Street fame had strolled nonchalantly into the lost situation.

A carnival atmosphere was in full swing. Enterprising young entrepreneurs had set up a trestle table serving drinks along with homemade jams, pickles and cakes.

A man dressed in Lederhosen had assembled a full size alpine horn that looked like a giant mammoth tusk.

Moira conducted the daily exercising of her two ferrets on leads—Dastardly and Mutley. She was happily encouraging people to stroke them for free. It was like Russian ferret roulette: she knew they would only draw blood from one in 40 strokes, which is why she thoughtfully carried bandages and plasters stowed in her pockets for such eventualities.

Young men wearing track suit bottoms and bearing their brown lean torsos cycled battered children's bikes slightly too small for them with their long arms dangling down by their sides before grabbing the handlebars to pull wheelies whilst all the time staking out any good thieving opportunities.

A small group of winos occupied the single garden bench. Armed with the heavy artillery of cheap 3-litre plastic cider bottles, they were looking forward to a hard day's pounding and bestowing the wino wisdom only the wino possesses onto strangers.

A geezer wearing a full-on flight uniform and sunglasses like he was a top gun pilot had put another bird in the sky in the form of a drone, hoping to get some much needed reconnaissance footage of the camera shy Dusky Thrush. He was about to get his first taste of aerial combat experience. A bogey (remote controlled hostile pterodactyl) had entered his airspace.

A young woman had painted her face in the style of a comedy white-faced clown with exaggerated red nose and smiley mouth. She was wearing a baggy all-in-one yellow costume with large red buttons and an orange Afro wig. It would be unkind to say she looked like Ronald McDonald because there was a gentle vulnerability and femininity to her that just doesn't exist in the creepy hamburger mascot. Opportunistically, she shook a large bucket for a children's cancer charity like a money maraca. It was easier for people to feed the bucket than hold eye contact for too long with her broken soul.

A buzz broke out amongst the birders. The buzz was made up of a lot of disapproving "Oh Gods!" and "Look out, here he comes!" "That's all we need!" and a few hearty "For fuck sakes!" It was not a positive buzz. One birder sardonically parodied another great Welshman with, "Oh dear, how sad, never mind." You don't become the champion year-lister by being popular. To win a competition like that you needed one-upmanship—Barry had it in spades. Bribing boat skippers and pilots to fly or ferry his nearest competitors to the wrong islands or on one occasion to Norway, as well as sabotaging internal combustion engines to ensure a rival dipped out on listing a bird was amongst many of the gamesmanship tactics he deployed over his rivals to gain an advantage.

Yes, the legendary 'Birdman' had arrived, carrying his armour-plated marvelousness before him. He swashbuckled into the Garden with more swagger than Errol Flynn and Don Juan combined. Barry could hear the glorious panpipes of his importance playing him into the Garden Square like the arrival of the Birdman of Sheba. Anybody would think he had a private audience with Dusky and was running late. "Come on, come on, get out of my way," said the de facto leader of birders, moving to take up his rightful place at the front of the viewing position. Barry quickly began to grip off about the rare birds he had listed due to his superior bird craft; it was like the bird catcher Papageno's opening aria from Mozart's *The Magic Flute*:

> I am a lad of widespread fame
> And Barry Jones is my name
> To tell the truth in simple words
> I am the best at listing birds—

# PORTRAIT OF DAVE

The square had become a warm, promising fire for company. A chartered holiday destination for the lonely in search of ears to listen:

"I lost my Ted last year after 60 years of marriage, he was a lovely man," said an old women in the general direction of ears.

"You must miss him terribly," replied a female birder, putting down her binoculars. She didn't know it yet but she was about to sacrifice an hour of her hobby to the story of her life. If there were any justice in this world her kindness would have been rewarded. There wasn't. You could hear this conversation repeated again on Christmas Day, on the forsaken circuit, at her local supermarket as she was shopping for fresh companionship to put in her basket. It was nearly always out of stock. Her loneliness would wander for months on end without finding company. There was no training for loneliness. The lonely didn't practice sleeping on their own before loneliness fell upon them—that was a big mistake.

Dave was lonely. He lost his wife when she choked to death on a fish bone; some say she got a lucky break. She loved her husband. She couldn't say it because she was too busy choking to death, but she would love him again in the afterlife and the life after that. She can't wait for Dave to die so she can be with him again. Not everybody is as lucky as Dave's wife. A lot of folk are going to be disappointed in the new afterlife that they didn't get on with getting divorced in their previous life. They're just going to end up taking the misery with them and telling their spouse for eternity they love them when they don't.

Dave was swarthy, possessing the hard, intimidating facial features of a mobster with a flat crooked nose and a large granite forehead carved with frown furrows so deep you could have grown cabbages in them; only his hands matched the proportions of his head. At school Dave was called Monkey Features, which was just about an A+ for description.

Lucien Freud would have wanted to stop Monkey Features in the street and beg him to return to his studio for a sitting with the promise of free bananas. Lucien Freud would have dreamt of a face like his. The art world is a poorer place without the Portrait of Dave.

Dave was endowed with a keen vexatiousness. He was a precocious moaner, reminding us that not all the lonely are in need of our sympathy. Many lonely people get the loneliness they deserve. Queues were the natural moaning ground for Dave's virtuoso moaning performances. He liked nothing more than a good old fashioned English queue, whether it was at the post office, petrol station, doctors waiting room or airline check in—wherever, as long as he could get his hands on a queue, he wasn't fussy. Dave would purposefully seek out the longest wait—he disliked it when rare acts of efficiency and organisation thwarted his whingeing—"Would you like to come across to this check-in sir?" Once happily in line he was the undisputed King Tut of Tutting, Sultan of Sighing, Mutt of Muttering, Grand Huff of Huffing, Sheik of Head Shaking.

Like all master grumblers he would warm up with barely audible incomprehensible muttering to himself—

this was the equivalent of switching on the grumbling engine. His happiest huffing ground was the supermarket. The supermarket could always be relied upon to consistently deliver the moaning goods. It was like a favourite riffle in a river that always offered up a good fish when everywhere else was deathly quiet:

A barcode wouldn't scan—"Huh!"

The receipt machine had run out of paper—"Tut-Huh!"

The flashing supervisor light had been engaged for help but the response time was not as quick as a Formula 1 pit stop crew replacing four tyres —"Tut-Tut!"

A declined credit card—"Tut-Tut-Tut!"

A woman produced more discount vouchers than a pack of playing cards—none of which were valid after a lengthy inspection—multiple head shakes—"Tut-Huh!"

A man with arthritis and hands like shaking root vegetables struggled slowly to count out the change from his wallet—"Huhhhh!"

A checkout lady and female customer were engaged in a full-blown conversation concerning their mutual love for holidaying in Kefalonia. "I'm sorry," Dave would say sarcastically, "we're not holding you up, are we?"

Dave loved nothing more than when being able to radicalise other disgruntled members of the public to his brand of tutting terrorism. In this regard there was no shortage of willing recruits. Dave had been responsible for many incidences of slow hand clapping, choruses of 'why are we waiting,' and sit-ins.

Dave was stood amongst the twitchers, birders, birdwatchers and curious members of the public, or as Dave would describe them—a bunch of wankers. New birders were arriving excitedly on the birding scene all the time. Dave annoyingly just caught the punch line end of a joke, "Have you got something other than rhubarb!" that had a good many people roaring with laughter. Dave earwigged in on some of the conversations going on around him with pre-vexation excitement and a wolfish grin like he knew something these wankers didn't:

"What do you do for a living?" said a male member of the human race innocently to a female birder he'd been flirting with.

"I won't be defined by my occupation!" she said waspishly, delighted to have been offended at last and making her day. Without free speech, her life, like a growing number of others, would never derive the slightest pleasure. General conversation was definitely down on previous years, much to the annoyance of the wanting-to-be-offended. Many of the people in the Garden were sensibly censoring themselves for fear of insulting or shaming anyone. Many but not all:

"Where was the last sighting?"

"See the big green tree?"

"Yep."

"Go up the trunk and take the first major branch on the right."

"Heard any good bird jokes recently?"

"My wife told me to stop impersonating a flamingo. I had to put my foot down!"

"Ha-ha, ok now where?"

"Follow the branch line all the way to the end."

"I can't see anything..."

"Ruth, you remember last week me getting stung by that hornet on Hackney Marshes?"

"Yes," said Ruth, "I felt sorry for you."

"No need," said the hornet victim. "You're not going to believe this Ruth, you're not going to believe this!" she repeated in a hushed excited tone.

"What?"

"Every night since I've been woken in the early hours having experienced the most thunderous multiple orgasms of my life!" she whispered.

"Lucky cow," said Ruth laughing.

"What am I going to do when the effect of the horny hornet sting wears off?"

"Get stung again! I'm going to join you!" said Ruth sensibly seizing the orgasm opportunity of a lifetime.

"I can't see anything..."

"Where can we buy hornets..."

"Can you believe the new Doctor Who is a woman?" said one of the winos with disgruntled Whoverian wino bench wisdom upon him.

"Disgraceful, the BBC should hang their heads in shame!" said his cider friend supportively.

"I've never sided with the Daleks before, but I hope they capture her Time-Ladyship and Dalek gang bang her bareback! That will teach them a well deserved lesson!" he replied vehemently.

"That's not funny! It's disgusting! How can you wish to see an innocent woman raped! You should be ashamed of yourselves!" said a bird-woman ignorant of the Daleks' lack of gender and a penis to carry out such an atrocity.

"YOU WILL BE INSEMINATED!" replied the cider man to the bird-woman.

"INSEMINATE! INSEMINATE! INSEMINATE!" ordered the remaining cider Daleks.

"I can't see anything..."

"There she blows!" shouted Dave, unable to contain himself any longer, pointing to a nearby cypress tree and causing a flurry of excited optical activity in the direction of his finger as the lenses swivelled around.

"I can't see it."

"2 o'clock," said Dave pointing his arm again. "2 o'clock," he repeated, as if identifying enemy aircraft before adding, "Bird ahoy!"

"Somebody should tell Captain Ahab it's a bird not fucking Moby Dick!"

Never before had so many eyes gazed upon the cypress tree—it blushed a darker shade of green.

"All I've got is a trash bird," said a bird lover, referring to a pigeon flapping around noisily whilst it found a branch to take its weight. It just wanted to get comfortable and carry on thinking beautiful burden-free pigeon thoughts.

"Hey, watch your mouth, that homing pigeon's ancestors could have been flying heroes, winning the medal of valour by navigating over enemy territory to deliver a top secret message: "Get the fuck out of there, Jerry is coming"—a message that probably saved the lives of your forebears and resulted in your ungrateful birth. Show a little more respect!" said a patriot.

"According to legend, it was a flock of pigeons pecking on the salt deposits that led to the discovery of spa waters and their unusual healing effect," said a local historian, taking the side of the pigeon. This pigeon had royal blood.

"That pigeon ain't got no song, that pigeon," someone mixed in clearly suffering from bird fever and sorely in need of quenching their madness in the spa waters. He's got that look in his eye that at any moment he might break the line and run out courageously to the cheering of his comrades on a suicidal mission to retrieve an injured soldier on his shoulders, only to be shot in cold blood in the back on his return and for the cheering to be silenced.

"Are you sure you saw it, mate?"

"I know a Husky Thrush when I see one," said Dave.

"Dusky Thrush," a stickler corrected him before adding: "Did it look like this?" showing him a picture of the bird in his bird guide.

"The spitting image but slightly bigger," replied Dave.

"There she blows!" repeated Captain Ahab, once again unable to help himself, but this time pointing up at the pterodactyl menacingly circling the turkey oak. "It's your lucky day, I bet you've never put one of those rare bad boys in your bird book! It's like fucking Jurassic Park in here," he laughed.

"That's me done for the day, not much to this birding lark, if you will excuse the pun," Dave vexed cheerily, before he headed off in the direction of the young capitalists for a well-earned cup of tea and slice of cake. As he approached, his heart warmed further with the sight of the refreshments queue.

# MR WIND

The strongest ever gust of wind recorded in Cheltenhamshire was 93 mph. 'Mr Wind' as he was known locally, had blown into the Garden party packing a large noisy gas-powered 185 mph backpack leaf blower. This left him with something to spare over the winds in these neck of the woods. Mr Wind had dominion over the wind.

Mr Wind was wearing ear defenders; as the leaves scatter danced before him, all the self-proclaimed King of Leaves could hear was the happy sweet love song of air singing inside his head. This time of year was slim pickings. He was waiting impatiently for the first christened storms of the autumn season or even better a hurricane to arrive. Mr Wind had a lot of respect for the masculine wind and the feeling was mutual. He liked his wind aggressive. The wind was his hero in the sky. Not the gentle summer winds that fall asleep in the trees and talk softly with them. Stuff that. Give him the wind that shouts, and strips the trees of their summer rank; a wind that ties trees up and tortures them for their leaves, that shreds their clothing. A dispossessing wind is what his heart desires.

Whilst the start of the Red Grouse season—The Glorious Twelfth (August) is well known—the official start of the leaf-blowing season—The Resplendent First (November)—is less so. Some blowers like Mr Wind can't wait that long: their leaf blowing addiction is just too strong. He would blow illegally.

Mr Wind was an unpopular menace. Last year's community spirited 'we're all in it together' weekend leaf clean-up by the residents had produced four large, impressive, golden leaf pyramids worthy of a place in the Valley of the Kings, ready for the council to collect on Monday morning.

That was just too much temptation for a man with such strong leaf cravings. Mr Wind paced up and down his first floor flat that looked directly out of his window onto the Garden Square. He watched the hard raking work of his fellow residents whilst he chain smoked cigarettes. His hands shook with the need for his leaf fix, *come on come on,* he said to himself under his trembling lips. He was like a cat on a hot tin roof. After the residents had returned home weary but satisfied with their day's community work, and darkness had bedded itself into the square, Mr Wind emerged like a tomb raider from the shadows.

Wet weather keeps the leaves down, clips their wings, grounds the blower's hobby. That weekend the weather had been dry and cold, crisping the leaf harvest to perfection. This was the cream of the vintage leaf crop. It didn't get much better than this. It was one hell of a leaf-rush for Mr Wind. His leaf-blowing spree went on until he ran out of leaf blowing ammunition. Why is he doing it? The answer, my friends, is *blowin' in the wind, the answer is blowin' in the wind...*

# T MINUS 13 VERSES

A man with a large green winged macaw parrot on his shoulder had arrived seeking attention from his fellow bird lovers to share his parrot passion. He figured it was just like a car rally but for birds. An attractive middle-aged couple were in town for the literature festival with two prize front row tickets to watch Stephen Fry at the Town Hall. They had stumbled on the rare-bird gathering whilst out enjoying the unseasonable weather and admiring the fine Regency architecture with a guide to Cheltenhamshire in their hands.

"What's its name?" asked the welcome literary strangers.

"Victor Hugo," said Macaw Man, delighted with some attention straight off the bat.

"He's one of my favourite writers," said the woman with an hourglass figure gushingly before continuing: "Did you know he was a podophile?" Literature types have a habit of showing off their knowledge. Macaw Man didn't look comfortable with this rhetorical question; if he had known Victor Hugo was a podophile he would never have chosen the name.

"No, I didn't know that," he replied disgustedly.

"My husband is a bit of a podophile himself," she said, laughing.

"Is he?" said Macaw Man, alarmed and not seeing the funny side.

"Does it talk?" said the podophile husband, shaking his

head affectionately at his wife.

"Every line of *Les Miserables*," said the bird owner, relieved to get the conversation back on track but wishing for a better audience. Right on cue Victor spoke:

"If I speak (squawk) I am condemned. If I stay silent (squawk), I am damned!"

"How charming," said the woman, impressed.

"We're going on Britain's Got Talent next spring."

The couple looked blankly at him.

"Do you like poetry?" he asked, moving back onto their wavelength.

"Oh yes," they both replied enthusiastically.

"Excellent," he said, producing a scroll of paper from his coat pocket quick as a magician.

"13 Verses for Victor," he said, becoming serious and clearing his throat.

"Squawk! 'There is something more terrible than a hell of suffering—a hell of boredom,'" quoted the parrot prophetically.

They would never have endured 13 Verses for Victor if they'd known how quickly the future was running out for them.

Back at cider HQ, one of the senior 'ciderians,' had, like a dangerous missionary, left the sanctuary of the 'church' bench to minister the wino wisdom to a tall gentleman wearing a magnolia Panama hat that had excitedly caught his attention standing out from the birding crowd. The wino saw himself as a leading connoisseur in matters of dress, having once owned a highly respectable gentlemen outfitters before hard retail times fell upon him. Any man wearing a Fedora Panama hat must be in need of his company was the logic that brought them together:

"If I'm not mistaken, is that not a rare Montecristi Panama you're wearing, sir?" asked the wino reverently.

"It is," said the man in the Panama hat with some surprise and all the Panama hat civility you would expect from a man wearing a Panama hat.

"A true work of art, a masterpiece of sublime beauty, made, if I'm not mistaken, at the hands of the master weaver signor Cristi himself, a man comparable with Faberge and Stradivarius," said the wino with distilled apple affectation and bloodshot eyes, taking a large slug to calm his hat emotions. 'The Hat' looked down on the stranger, impressed with his knowledge of his hat before replying informatively:

"Five thousand weaves per inch and twelve months to handmake according to family folklore."

"A family heirloom passed lovingly down the generations?" inquired the wino.

"Yes, my great-grandfather acquired it whilst British Ambassador to Ecuador."

"You have a fine shaped head for the hat sir, as if you were born for the hat. It must feel very special to wear that hat."

"Thank you, it does make me feel very good," said 'The Hat' truthfully.

"Of course it does! When you wear that hat good things happen, do they not? It has brought you luck, I wager? Happiness? Successful career? Pretty wife? Children? Good health?"

"I have been very lucky in life," said 'The Hat' reflectively and modestly.

"Of course you have! Of course you have! The hat has seen to that."

"I've worked hard for what I have," said 'The Hat', distancing his fortune from his headwear.

"You've heard of the saying 'to weave magic'?" asked the wino mysteriously.

"Yes," replied 'The Hat'.

"It was said that Cristi was a weaver of Ecuadorian magic. He made incantations as he wove your very hat, imbuing it with luck and good fortune."

"I don't believe in superstitions, but hopefully it will bring me luck with this reclusive Dusky Thrush!" said 'The Hat' with the perfect polite segue to return to his binoculars and away from shaggy cider stories.

Telling the wino to fuck off was never an option for a gentleman wearing a rare Panama hat. Giles, for that was the name of the wino, took some time out from his ministering to top up his cider levels. As he did so the lucky Fedora hat owner recommenced his hobby. How different his life would have been if he'd owned that Fedora, thought Giles as he stared covetously at the fabulous hat.

# THE STRAWBERRY RIVER

The unknown poet had taken Wongo over to the Garden for his daily second walkies. You could set your watch by it. Benny the Twitch did.

Today was the unknown poet's wife's birthday. Happy Birthday. He'd booked a table at their favourite restaurant for that night at 7.30. In her honour he'd written a short poem on a birthday card that was resting inside his coat pocket ready to romantically hand to her over a glass of prosecco. He didn't know it but he was about to fulfil a life-long ambition in becoming a published poet. The bummer is a national newspaper would publish it posthumously after his death. Mrs Wongo would read the poem on her own with tears of grief running down her face whilst Wongo looked on happily.

## THE STRAWBERRY RIVER

There is a strawberry river
That flows inside of me,
Carrying midsummer strawberryness
That makes the strawberry strawbird sing.
There is a strawberry river
That flows inside of me,
With a tide of warm strawberry memory
Running into a strawberry sea.
Its source—your strawberry lips
Our very first kiss.

# FLASH GORDON

Wellington Square and the surrounding Pittville Park area of Cheltenhamshire was a hotspot for flashers. Flashing had become a popular hobby for some. Most local women at one time or another in their lives had been flashed at multiple times. The ones that hadn't felt bad about it, they spent a lot of time worrying why. Flashing was no big deal anymore. If you wanted to see a flasher you knew where to come. There were increasingly a growing number of female flashers on the flashing scene. Men were outraged.

Gordon was a well-known celebrity flasher in these parts. Gordon liked to creatively combine his flashing with streaking. He protected his real identity by wearing handmade painted silicone masks of the famous. He made them himself with great skill using real hair.

It took Gordon exactly three months to make a mask; it really was a work of art, and you wouldn't know Gordon was wearing a mask—it being completely lifelike. It was all part of the ritual he so enjoyed. His flashing was on a 3-month cycle. He was like a flashing comet orbiting the neighbourhood. Gordon was the flasher people wanted to see most. Gordon had a touch of flashing class—he was an artist and the best flasher in Cheltenhamshire bar none, a fact that filled him with a certain amount of pride and satisfaction. So far, David Beckham, Sir Ian McKellan, Ricky Gervais, Jeremy Corbyn, and Dame Judy Dench had all been spotted waving their todger's in the neighbourhood. It was quite an honour to be flashed at by the best Britain had to offer. You knew you had made it in society if Flash Gordon was stealing your identity. Given the lifelike nature of the masks, the impersonated all needed rock solid alibis, even Dame Judy!

Each flash had to be ritually accompanied with a new mask. This was going to be Gordon's swansong before he hung up his masks for the final time. One day in the future his masks are going to turn up on the Antiques Roadshow—"I was just clearing out my fathers attic..." They will fetch a small fortune at auction. Gordon wanted to go out on a high, retire at the peak of his flashing powers. He was taking a big risk with this final farewell daytime flash.

Gordon, when he's not flashing, was a highly respectable resident of Wellington Square and retired commodities trader. He lived with his unsuspecting wife in the north-eastern corner of the square in an imposing gothic style Old Rectory that looked like it was built exclusively to home Dracula. It stood in complete contrast to the huddle of Regency and Victorian houses beside it. It was like a Victorian gothic punk rocker. It was constructed of red brick with purple brick banding. It had an attractive tile roof with two tall brick ridge stacks at either end. They were crying out for remote controlled bats to be circling them. Its three gables were decorated with beautiful finials and bargeboards. The mullion windows should have had pumpkins glowing with candles in them and spiders hanging down. The arched central voussoir entrance to the house would have any trick-or-treaters trembling by the time they reached its pointed plank door. It was not surprising that the residents of this wonderful home were known locally as the Count and Countess.

Count Flashula was about to strike again.

He can't wait to run around waving his Moby Dick at strangers whilst accompanying it with some strange guttural panting sounds that he performed purely for his own amusement just to witness the bemused faces of his victims. You've got your life, Gordon had his.

# THE CUCKOO OF AWARENESS (III)

"Get a good nights sleep tonight Tom, tomorrow will be the Longest Day."

"I take it what you mean by that is that tomorrow it's all going tits-up?"

"The biggest hooters-up of all time."

"And so it actually truly comes to pass?"

"Right in front of our eyes."

"You don't seem in the slightest bit worried."

"Whatever IS, is right Tom."

"Are you out of your cuckoo catchphrase mind?"

"Tom, my fine non-feathered friend, that was a quote taken from the Pope himself."

"Now hopefully you can see why I'm an atheist fundamentalist."

"Not that Pope Tom, THE Pope, Popey to me, the great English poet Alexander Pope:

*All nature is but art, unknown to thee;*
*All chance, direction, which thou canst not see;*
*All discord, harmony, not understood;*
*All partial evil, universal good:*
*And, spite of pride, in erring reason's spite,*
*One truth is clear, Whatever is, is right."*

"My world has literally collapsed around me, nearly all my neighbours are, if you will forgive the expression, cuckoo, and tomorrow I set my alarm clock for 7am, the am being short for Armageddon, and you would have me believe, like the insanely optimistic Dr Pangloss, that in spite of all human suffering—'everything is for the best in the best of all possible worlds…'?"

"Nothing we can do, Tom, can make it go any better."

"Try making a better world!"

"You've not heard my Voltaire story."

"I'd like to keep it that way."

"In that case, Tom, you'd better set your alarm for 5 Armageddon, we have a lot of catching up to do."

"This desk job is killing me. Tomorrow you can't just expect me to stand idly by and watch guiltily risk-free whilst innocent creatures die. I'm ready to do my bit in violent combat; I'm requesting you transfer me to the front line."

"Request denied."

"You'd make a coward of me?"

"'To hold a pen is to be at war,' Tom."

"Your man Voltaire again. You're more of a magpie than a cuckoo!"

"Nothing is more important than bearing witness, to tell the true stories of these people, furthermore you would die within seconds."

"Transfer request withdrawn."

"Accepted."

"Voltaire's story?"

"To cut a long story short—"

"Please do."

"It was after his triumphant return to Paris, he confessed to me, 'Do you know, my dearest friend, I think my Doctor Pangloss was right all along, 'everything is for the best in the best of all possible worlds'."

"They should have kept him locked in the Bastille!"

"Good night, Tom."

# PART THREE

# FRIDGE

Benny the Twitch was sat in the getaway car eagerly looking forward to dealing with Wongo and Mr Wongo personally. Wongo the Wonder Dog was an endangered species—although what species he actually was nobody really knew. His wondrous life was in peril.

Benny's favourite professional hood, 'The Refrigerator' or 'Fridge' for short, making any further description superfluous, had squeezed himself out of the car. The Fridge's father and grandfather had worked with distinction for the Whitechapel family firm. Fridge was a chip off the old ice block. His father was known as the 'Tumble Dryer' and his grandfather as the 'Cooker'. He came from a long line of large domestic appliances.

Fridge entered the square as inconspicuous as a giant gladiator dressed in a finely tailor-made suit can be. The tailor had to use a stool to measure this monster—it was a tidy bit of business—he would miss the Fridge. To be on the safe side Fridge was going to bind all four gates to cut of any means of escape for Wongo and the unknown poet. This may have been a simple job, made even simpler by the welcome cover of the rare-bird commotion, but Fridge prided himself on his attention to detail. He had crystal clear instructions to retrieve the targets alive. Before binding the final gate he courteously held it open for Big Bird to exit, who, with Sesame Street politeness, nodded her yellow beak in appreciation.

# HALL OF FAMER

Up to now Mrs Eva Gittler had made very few bad decisions in her most exemplary life.

She was about to make up for that.

If you collected all the bad decisions made since bad decision records began, this was a hall of famer. It was worthy of standing alongside Hitler's decision to invade Russia, filling the Hindenburg full of hydrogen and the memory of the twelve publishers who, having read *Harry Potter and the Philosopher's Stone*, decided to reject it.

History would not be kind to Mrs Gittler.

She innocently believed she was the wife of a well-respected civil servant, not a tyrant.

She wouldn't be the last woman to unwittingly marry a monster.

Eva was kind. Her eyes and ears sucked up the condition of strangers, family and friends, processed them through her caring body, and returned to them love, gentleness and wise counsel. She spent so much time thinking of others and helping them that her ego never woke to twist her life; she went through life serenely, much loved by everybody. If you will forgive the indulgence in paraphrasing words from my own rather wonderfull ego-free cuckoo song: she avoided the 'striving sickness', her 'spontaneity was constantly present.'

Eva Gittler had a special gift for kindness.

There are too many days that arrive with a deficit of love.

When the molecules of the day contain more cruelty than love, despair than hope, and stupidity than intelligence, when days are overrun by too much grief, when too many innocent children die, then such a day is upon us.

They arrive like a sinister spaceship made of black cancer—an illness sat in the sky— they make you feel sick, like a letter from the war office dropping through your letter box.

Scrambled from churches, synagogues and mosques—squadrons of well meaning prayers get sent to intercept it—to give strength to leaders—to make it go away. They bounce disdainfully off the thick-skinned hull of its prayer deflector shield into the prayersphere, the graveyard of unanswered prayers.

If only the kindness of Eva Gittler and others like her could rise up.

Rise up in rebellion.

Rise up in a contagion of kindness.

History would be unkind to Eva Gittler.

Eva's grave would be desecrated by hatred.

Someone would spray paint the word WHORE on her broken gravestone.

That someone was her best friend. It would turn out to be one of the more complimentary pieces of graffiti.

Kindness uprisings are hard to get off the ground.

The miscarriage of justice that would fall on the lovely Eva Gittler was a sacrifice worth making.

Fortunately, Wellington Square wasn't going to stand for it anymore; it was going to fight back and give the day some much-needed molecules of love, hope and intelligence.

Prayers would be answered.

Wellington Square is going to rise up!

It's going to rise up with glorious cheerleading grandeur.

Go, Wellington Square!

We are getting ahead of ourselves.

The mysterious air traffic controller warmly welcomed the black swans of Eva Gittler's very bad decision.

It was such a pleasant afternoon that Mrs G thought it would be a super idea to send over all their guests to the party marquee to see her husband armed with drinks and canapés whilst she got on with putting the final touches to the festivities for her husband's retirement party. She knew Louis would love proudly holding court as King Dusky Thrush. Eva was still a little miffed with him for requisitioning her brand new marquee that she had intended to use in their garden for the party; they may as well put it to the use it was meant for, she thought.

This was the equivalent of sending the entire royal family and heirs in disguise on a walking holiday in rural Afghanistan without their personal protection officers. In fact it was worse than this, as the hatred the Cheltshireons had for the Highways & Parking team far outweighed that of the Taliban for the Western world.

# MOOM MONSTERS (IV)

There was plenty of room at the hill inn. The entire Moom population in the old world had returned to Murria. They were very tired from their journey and slept all night and well into the afternoon of the next day, which suggested they must have travelled from far, far away. Fortunately, the Moom didn't snore like the snorting snoring monster that is your mum! Which is just as well because if they did they wouldn't just keep me awake all night like Mummy, they would keep awake the entire city!

The Mu slept well. As they returned to the city and their homes, everything was reassuringly in place: the stars in the sky and the Mooms in residence on the high hills with their glowing golden lights. There was moonlight and Moomlight and everyone slept safely and happily under them. Some of them had very bad heads the next day from enjoying themselves too much.

Now, Freddie, I don't know about you but I think it's about time we talked about the Wily-Wily! You remember that's the other name for the Mooms. Let me tell you how they came by this name.

The Wily-Wily is also the name the Mu gave to a wind. It was not a good wind that filled ships' sails, flew kites, dried clothes, turned windmills or whispered to the trees and ruffled hair. The Wily-Wily was a frightening wind; a cold wind that came from the East. The Wily-Wily would scare you, Freddie, make you tremble and your teeth chatter, but a far greater horror resided in the East, in the new Kingdom of Hex. The old good-hearted King had long since been murdered and replaced by the House of Hex—the evil warlock Darken Hemlock and his twin sister Sarin Hemlock now ruled over the most powerful kingdom in the old world.

It was rumoured that far to the east of Murria the spiteful sorcerers had cast a spell to silence all the blackbirds from singing, just for fun. Imagine a place without that beauty to listen to.

Now, you probably imagine that Darken & Sarin wore baggy robes and pointy hats, carried magic wands or staffs, rode around on broomsticks and possessed a great white beard or crooked nose, had a pet black cat and were hated by their people. You'd be wrong on all counts. Darken & Sarin's great-grandwarlock, Sulfur Hemlock, was the last wizard to look like a traditional wizard. A statue of the old wizard stood proudly in the palace of Hex, brandishing his staff, looking like a true wizard! Times and fashion had moved on. Mind you, it didn't mean they wore T-shirts with the words ABRACADABRA written on them! Sarin & Darken wore finely tailored clothing made from the shed skin of the rare Giant Black Toad. It was the darkest, lightest and strongest material ever known—so dark that it absorbed 100 percent of light and 100 times stronger than steel. Their clothes were a cross between a Chinese changshan and cheongsam for women, and the Japanese kimono with the addition of hoodies. Sulfur's sandals were replaced with boots made from the same material. Evil had never looked so good on the handsome twins.

The Hexicans—for that was the name of the people of Hex, loved their rulers, for they had made them all extremely wealthy. Hex was the first ever country to give birth to an industrial revolution. Sarin & Darken granted licences to the newly conferred Barons of Hex to manufacture their potions and spell kits on an unprecedented scale for sale. They were magic business baron magnets.

In all there were six Barons of Hex:

The Red Baron, or the love baron as he was known, responsible for spells & potions of love and fertility; a lot of people in the world were searching for love and wanted children; the Red Baron could even mend a broken heart. The Red Baron was the busiest Baron—his best seller was his love potion no 7.

The White Baroness—she was responsible for spells & potions that brought health and healing. I guess she was the equivalent of a private Witch Doctor. If you had a toothache or arthritis like Grandma, or even something fatal, the White Baroness was your woman, providing you had a private healthcare policy with her and kept up the payments!

The Green Baron—he was responsible for spells that delivered financial fortune, luck, and success. The only problem was that you had to be rich, lucky or successful just to afford to buy the Green Baron's spells!

The Blue Baroness—also known as the Charm Baron, was the provider of amulets that took the form of necklaces, brooches, pendants and rings. The amulets were shaped with ancient symbols and would often contain crystals, gems or simple stones that when worn close to your body gave the wearer good luck and protection. If you were afraid of the Big Bad Wolf, the Bogeyman, Vampires and Evil Spirits—let's face it, who isn't—then you needed to buy some Blue Baroness Jewellery!

The Purple Baron—the most wealthy and profitable of the Barons. He delivered spells that jinxed, cursed, killed and revenged. These spells were the most profitable and expensive, they literally changed hands for a king's ransom.

Last but not least there was the Black Baron. The Black Baron was the favourite Baron of Darken & Sarin. His name was Zagan Morfran but was known simply and chillingly as Morfran. Morfran was the Minister of State Security for Hex. He was the most feared and malevolent of men; even his fellow Barons distrusted him.

Competition was fierce between the Barons. The buildings that manufactured the magic were branded in the individual Barons' corporate house colours, as were the ships' sails that sailed from the great capital city port of Hexopolis to deliver the magic. The people of Hex had all the best positions and jobs whilst slaves from other lands had the most dangerous work and were treated very badly. Hexopolis was an exotic cauldron of life; the noise and colour filled the senses to over brimming. It was both dangerous and exciting. The Hexicans were great importers as well as exporters. The Barons needed raw and living materials for their spells that weren't all readily available in their own land. Seeds, bark and berries, roots and reptiles; herbs, algae and amphibians; fungi and fish, wax and sap. Add to this diamonds, silver, gold and crystals, not to mention all manner of other strange and wonderful creatures and substances. These were just the tip of the animal, vegetable and mineral iceberg. Many of the spells were sadly cruelly brewed. Did I mention human body parts? Goods were traded far and wide. Many countries also grew rich from supplying the Hexicans. It would take a brave country not to trade with the Hexicans and face the wrath of Darken & Sarin—very brave.

The demand for their witchcraft & wizardry far outstripped the supply. The spell business was booming. The Hexican sales network grew and grew to more and more lands taking orders from individuals and rulers. Great legions of Crows would fly back and forth with orders to the Barons' factories for processing. All spells were copyrighted, could only be used once and their effects would last just a short period of time, leading to lucrative repeat prescriptions. The Hexicans didn't care that the poor could not afford to buy the potions to save their families from plagues and illnesses and that many people would die in wars and vendettas. They would sell their magical wares to the highest bidder—business was business and the price was the price. Many nations were in debt to the Kingdom of Hex from long wars, crippled by the interest charges made by the Purple Baron. The Purple Baron would happily supply both enemy armies at the same time. Wars were good for profits. The dark agents of Hex under the command of Morfran would seek out and kill individuals that didn't pay their bills. Which reminds me I have a few to pay myself! I never did tell you how the Wily-Wily got their name, did I?

# I LOVE WHEELBARROW

Aloysius had lost all sense of time, completely forgetting about the party. Red-faced, he'd been having a heated discussion with the 'Birdman' about the state of birding affairs in his marquee garden tent HQ. Just as he thought matters couldn't get any worse, and much to the delight of the media, Sitting Bull, dressed in full battle dress, led his two thousand strong brave warriors marching into the Garden, breaching the disgruntled birder perimeter, chanting and holding their banners aloft; only the winos cheered loudly with merriment, raising their cider bottles in approval.

"Hey hey! Ho ho! Twitchers have got to go! Say it loud! Say it clear! Dusky Thrush not welcome here!"

It was an impressive turnout. News of the demonstration had quickly spread to the professional protestors, anarchists, activists and nut jobs. Taking out their handmade banners and placards was meat and protest drink to these amigos. Most of them had subscribed to the protest hotline that texted them news of the latest demonstration. Some of them didn't have a clue what the hell they were demonstrating about—for them it was the camaraderie of taking part that mattered. A tall slim guy with a body the colour of milk was carrying a life-size wooden crucifix wearing just a loincloth. Last week he was at an anti badger cull demo. Another gangly brother of the human race with just as much right as anybody else to breathe planet Earth's indiscriminating air, carried a sign proclaiming: "I'M THE DADDY" whilst dressed as a Daddy Long Legs, looking like a large mosquito with six legs. The fascists and anti-fascists were united in their distaste for The Daddy. They were here to take their protesting seriously. There was no place for a grown man dressed as a Daddy Long Legs in the Cultural Revolution they yearned for. Brady didn't recognise the vast majority of the faces but he was pleased they were getting in on the act in such large numbers. It was an eclectic mix of revolutionaries all with just causes in their hearts.

There were many hundreds of LGBT rainbow flags flying proudly. At the end of one of the rainbow flags was a man proudly counterbalancing their position, holding aloft a banner offering divine gold intervention:

'HOMO SEX IS SIN—CHRIST CAN SET YOU FREE!'
The pick of the placard pops went like this:
'ALL BIRDERS ARE BASTARDS!'
'I LOVE WHEELBARROW!'
'GOD HATES BIRDERS!'
'STOP PREMATURE CHRISTMAS SHOPPING!'
'GANDALF WOULDN'T LET THIS SHIT HAPPEN!'
'HERE FOR VIOLENCE!'
'JESUS WILL SWEEP AWAY GUANTANAMO!'
'FIRST DOBBY DIES NOW THIS!'
'DEFROST THOROUGHLY BEFORE USE.'
'ARM THE DOLPHINS!'
'DELETE YOUR BROWSING HISTORY!'
'VOTE PEOPLE AGAINST BUREAUCRACY.'
'BAD DOBBY! BAD DOBBY! BAD!'
'WHAT DO WE WANT?
MINIATURIZATION

WHEN DO WE WANT IT?

NOW.'


Brady raised his Tomahawk above his head—his braves fell silent. "Where is your Chief?" he said with great authority. The birders pointed somewhat bemused in the direction of the marquee. By now Jones and Gittler were outside looking on in astonishment. Brady walked straight past them into the 'Tepee'—Dave couldn't help himself, shouting helpfully, "You wanna sort them out Wayward!" Jones and Gittler returned to the tent to find Brady waiting for them sat legs crossed on the floor.

"My name is Sitting Bull, I come in peace, please join me."

Jones looked at his blonde hair and moustache before commenting dryly, "You look more like General Custer than Sitting Bull."

"I defeated Yellow Beard at the battle of Little Bighorn," said Sitting Bull factually. Jones didn't need his former military training to quickly realise Brady was a nut with no sense of humour and a tomahawk in his hand. Jones sat down opposite him and kept his mouth shut, happy to do as he was told for once in his life.

"Look, Bob," said Gittler with a crusty tone to his voice.

"Sit down," the Birdman advised authoritatively, patting the ground next to him. Gittler complied.

Brady took out his peace pipe and filled it with marijuana, lit it, took a big draft and passed it to Gittler whom, seeing the nod from the Birdman and desperate to do anything that would return the place to a semblance of normality, reluctantly inhaled the peace offering and instantly began coughing. The talks proceeded in an increasingly civilised manner with the peace pipe holding it all peacefully together. Despite this, the peace process was always doomed to break down. Jones and Gittler were never going to be able to agree to Bob's uncompromising and unrealistic demands for the birders to leave his reservation immediately.

Brady returned to lead his band of protesting brothers and sisters who had waited patiently for him. They were delighted when Bob once more struck up the protesting band: "Hey hey! Ho Ho!"

# PUBLIC SERVICE ANNOUNCEMENT

All day Cheltenhamshire FM had been broadcasting from Welly Square.

"Any sign of that there Dusky?" asked Dick from Winchcombe, ringing in to guess the year.

"Not a sausage."

"They wanna sprinkle some of my old lady's suet puddin' beneath that there tree, inedible to most humans, but the song thrushes in our garden luv my missus's suet puddin', can't get enough of it, mind you it does affect their singing voice sum-in rottun."

"I think he's gained the power of invisibility, Dick."

"He'll still come down for the suet, mark my word, you'll see it disappear as he eats it—dead giveaway."

"Any idea on the year, Dick?"

"Is it 2080?"

"Sorry, Dick, did you say 1980?"

"No, 2080."

"You can't guess a year in the future, Dick."

"The game is called the time tunnel ryte?"

"Yes but..."

"So am I ryte or rong?"

"Do you know what, Dick, it has been a long day, I'm going to give it to you."

"Get in my babee!"

The Doughnuts' secret station had been busy taking a keen eavesdropping interest in the life of Mr Whitechapel or the 'Rabbit' as they referred to him. He'd been on their watch-every-move radar for some time now. They didn't need to use much of their spycraft to hack into his mobile phone and computer and track him. The more they got to know the Twitch the more they despised him.

"Is the operative in the target area?" asked the controller seriously.

"Affirmative, 'Birdwatcher' Big Bird in place."

"Send it," instructed the controller coldly.

Alongside Benny the Twitch the Doughnuts had also been keeping a much more pleasurable interest in the adventures of Dusky. It was the prank that just kept on giving. The Doughnuts had long ago compromised the identities of Gittler's High Command and their unexpected and inexplicable arrival in the Garden sent a flutter of excitement and flurry of activity through their nerve centre. They couldn't believe their luck.

Intercepting signals is what these young cats did for a living. Hijacking the broadcast signals of radio stations and mobile phone networks was a walk in the intrusion park. A piece of paper was quickly handed to a Doughnut sat at some fancy looking electronic equipment on loan from GCHQ. The female radio operator cleared her throat before broadcasting live through a voice scrambler:

"We interrupt this broadcast to bring you a public service announcement from Wellington Square on behalf of the Guantanamo Liberation Army:

"Highways & Parking scum for killing! I repeat: Highways & Parking scum for killing! This is the duty of the hour! Rise up, fellow people of Cheltenhamshire!

"We interrupt..."

# A WALK ON THE WILD SIDE

The sensational rumours of Hawthorne's public coming-out spread at warp speed across social media networks and communities. There was a strange, detached, gossipy buzz around the ground.

It was in the lucky seventh minute of the second half that the chattering stopped and the curse of the Mummy was finally broken: a desperate goal line clearance from a corner ricocheted off Mummford's shin and squirmed uglily into the goal. After a split second of surprise—they had not celebrated a goal in seventeen hours of football—the Mummy's goal-scoring memory and that of the fans reset itself. Mummford had a foldable fez strapped to the inside of his socks—it had been there, redundant for a long time—like a condom in a wallet just waiting for the chance for action. He ran to the advertising hoarding behind the goal, put on his fez and delighted the fans with his trademark Egyptian sand dance, all while the fans sang:

"Way-oh-way-oh-way-ooo-aaa-ooo...

"Walk like an Egyptian

"Walk like an Egyptian."

The fans could sense the tide changing; the Condors were pushing forward in search of an equaliser with all the hallmarks of Hawthorne's attractive brand of football; their eyes were firmly on the match now, not the manager.

Then came the sweet thunder-thud of a perfectly timed Mummford volley from twenty yards, followed by the lightning of the ball hitting the net with a rippling force; such a zipping sound that not even a harp-playing angel could emulate. The sound went straight to the hearts of the fans behind the goal—the away team's diving goalkeeper didn't get the slightest touch to the ball, adding to its virgin perfection. Like a fly, the goalkeeper became entangled, helplessly caught in the web of the corner of the net. The fans went wild with sombrero-waving spider celebration; after the longest goal drought in living memory, the River Nile had now burst its banks:

"Way-oh-way-oh-way-ooo-aaa-ooo...

"Walk like an Egyptian

"Walk like an Egyptian

"Da da dada daddaa..."

The Cheltenhamshire fans were really getting behind their team, pushing them forward with song and cheer. They knew that the song that pushed them forward like no other was their famous club anthem, a song that can make the hairs on the back of your neck lie down. As the Condors poured forward in search of a winning goal, the fans belted it out from the terraces:

"Weeee carrrnt read and we carrnt rite,

"but that don't rearly materrr,

"we all come from Cheltenhamshire,

"and we can drive a tracter!

"Oo ahrr, oo ahrr, oo ahrrr, oo ahrrr, oo ahrrr!

"Cheltenhamshire la la la

"Cheltenhamshire la la la!

"Cheltenhamshire la la la

"Cheltenhamshire la la la!"

Hawthorne sensed the opposition were in full retreat as they defended deeper and deeper. With killer instincts, he substituted a midfield player to give Gary 'Fulch' Fulcher, a former academy player and attacking winger, his first team debut. The away fans' piss-taking was replaced with anxious glances at the clock and premature whistles for the ref to end the game. Deep into the last seconds of injury time—a mysterious time that sits beyond normal space-time and relativity—'Fulch' got in behind the defence to whip in a dangerous cross. It was dangerous in more ways than one. Perry Mummford, despite seeing their goalkeeper coming to punch the ball away, threw himself bravely head first at the ball, meeting it a split second before the goalkeeper. Mummford never heard the deafening roar and delirium of the crowd as the ball hit the back of the net. He was KO from the gloved punch intended for the ball, not his chin. Unable to walk like an Egyptian, Mummford was stretchered from the pitch, his long pale legs dangling over the edge of the stretcher, sportingly applauded by both sets of fans.

Concerned for the Mummy's wellbeing, Hawthorne instinctively walked onto the pitch, looking and dressed like a concerned mother to meet the stretcher-bearers coming off in full view of the fans and the world. Later, a leading sports columnist would write: "Hawthorne's courage has beckoned a new age of pluralism; it was one of the great liberating moments not only in the history of sport but in social history." From the terraces, increasing in volume and unity, the fans declared their position on Hawthorne:

"We said, hey Joe, take a walk on the wild side
"We said, hey Joe, take a walk on the wild side
"And the Cheltenhamshire fans say
"Doo doo doo doo doo doo doo doo doo

"Doo doo doo doo doo doo doo doo doo
"Doo doo doo doo doo doo doo doo doo
"Doo doo doo doo doo doo doo doo doo
"Doo doo doo doo doo doo doo doo doo
"Doo doo doo doo doo doo doo doo doo
"Doo doo doo doo doo doo doo doo doo dooooooo."

Hawthorne proudly saluted the fans in acknowledgement, providing the paparazzi with the perfect shot for the newspapers. The Condors played out the last minutes of the game, keeping the ball with style; every pass was greeted with a loud sombrero waving "OLÉ!" from the crowd before the referee blew his whistle with the distinctive trailing third blast to bring the game to an end. The away team manager shook Hawthorne's hand, wondering privately how it was going to look when they had the traditional drink together in the players' lounge. Hawthorne returned to the dressing room in time to see Mummford regain consciousness.

"Did we save the Hobbits?" said the heroic Mummy, clearly still concussed.

"We certainly did, Perry," said Hawthorne smiling. Outside, the Cheltenhamshire fans were still singing:

"Doo doo doo doo doo doo doo doo doo
"Doo doo doo doo doo doo doo doo doo
"Doo doo doo doo doo doo doo doo doo
"Doo doo doo doo doo doo doo doo doo
"Doo doo doo doo doo doo doo doo doo dooooooo."

# THE SECRETS OF THE RAINFOREST

The countdown to the start of the Battle of Wellington Square came to an end just as the yellow nurse was putting her knickers back on in the late afternoon. It came to an end at the precise time that Macaw Man finished the last unlucky line of his epic love poem—13 Verses for Victor, "For he knows the secrets of the rainforest."

It came to an end moments after Big Bird had left the Garden, Sitting Bull had returned to his braves and Perry Mummford had bravely thrown his head at Fulch's cross. It came to an end when the Guantanamo Liberation Army made their historic broadcast.

This was the moment the crows had foretold: the thunderstorm had brewed, the thunderclap was nigh, Black Swans were about to take to the sky!

The shockwave from the roar of the three thousand Cheltenhamshire Town fans' exuberant celebration of the Mummy's hattrick rolled into Wellington Square from Whaddon Road like thunder straight into the ears of the reclusive Dusky Thrush, stirring him enough to move into a visible position to see what the fuss was all about. As it did so, the flaparrazi opened up with a flurry of rapid fire optical shooting. Many of the birders and amateurs had not switched off their flashlights: it was like a Marilyn Monroe movie premiere.

# BIG BIRD

Having received the text to commence the mission, Big Bird waddled over to the car where Benny the Twitch was waiting for Fridge to return with Wongo and the Unknown Poet. He couldn't make his mind up on the brutal and agonising form of slow death he would deliver to them following the murder of John Denver and the considerable loss of his money. Roasting Wongo alive and making his owner eat him before placing him in an Iron Maiden he'd purchased from an antiquities sale at Christie's was high on the short list.

Big Bird knocked on the tinted rear window of the jam jar. The Twitch, wondering what this geezer was playing at, couldn't resist lowering the window. "F is for Vincent Van Gogh!" he said cockney pleased with himself, waving Big Bird away, laughing.

Big Bird removed her head and pulled her arms from the costume. Amelia Atkins blew some sticky strands of fine hair from her pretty face before smiling warmly at the gentleman and raising a shooter—"F is for Freddie, our beautiful son," she said. Benjamin Whitechapel had just enough time for his shoulders to twitch twice nervously and for the smirk to disappear from his mouth in the split second before Mrs Atkins calmly emptied a full magazine of retributive lead into the face and body of Benjamin Whitechapel, filling the jam jar with raspberry jam to the musical roar of the celebrating Condor fans.

Feeling as free as a bird, Amelia returned herself

calmly to her anthropomorphic canary disguise before heading for the short flightless walk home. As she walked, she wondered how she would ever be able to thank Mrs Whippy for helping her.

# DUSKY BITES THE DUST

The Count had undressed, placing his clothes into a small rucksack that he'd hidden the night before in one of the tree islands. All he had on was his favourite streaking trainers—no socks, the rucksack on his back containing his original clothing and of course a new mask. He did some professional streaker stretching and warmed up by sprinting on the spot. The last thing he wanted to do was pull a hamstring muscle.

With a mighty 'flash, a-ah'—the 45th President of the United States, Donald J Trump—broke cover for the final streaking performance of his life. He ran towards the turkey oak whilst flapping his arms up and down like he was trying to fly, before stopping briefly to add some crazy jester hopping movements from side to side. He then stood still, leant back slightly at the hips and pointed his pecker in the direction of the crowd whilst making his trademark guttural noise that carried a high tariff on the warped factor scale.

It didn't distract Peter. As the Dusky Thrush was posing like Marilyn Monroe for the cameras, Peter adjusted his scope, capturing the superstar in his deadly crosshairs. He pulled the trigger, the audible snapping sound adding to the camera noise and gunfire.

The Dusky Thrush fell like a stunt-bird from a burning tree building—it was dead before it hit the ground. Many of the birders rushed forward, determined to list Dusky dead or alive and get him posted on their Facebook page.

"He was still breathing when I listed him," one ghoul would lie.

Witnessing the cold-blooded assassination of Dusky was too much for the young man with pigeon fever who was already dangerously close to the edge.

"They killed Dusky, they killed Dusky!" he cried, pointing to the braves carrying incriminating anti-birder signs who were now cheering deliriously, shaking their placards, high fiving and fist pumping joyfully at the death of Dusky and the imminent end to the nightmare siege of their homes.

"DEATH TO THE BIRD KILLERS!" he screamed, running towards Sitting Bull's army armed only with a bad case of bird fever.

"DEATH TO THE CAT KILLERS!" screeched Cat Woman

"DEATH TO THE CAT KILLERS!" repeated Crazy Parrot.

# FAREWELL MR WONGO

Fridge would simply retrieve Wongo and the unknown poet with the minimum of force and take them back to the 'mota'. That was the plan. As all generals know, including the Duke of Wellington from whom the square takes its name, 'no plan survives contact with the enemy.'

Squadron Leader Drone was struggling to get the pterodactyl with its superior manoeuvrability of his tail. Not even the Red Baron could outfly the previously extinct flying reptile. He'd been concentrating so hard on defeating the dinosaur that he'd completely forgotten the golden Queensberry Rule—'Keep your hands up and protect yourself at all times.' That's what everyone else was doing as the fighting spread.

It was very unsportsmanlike of Mr Wind to fire a cheap-shot thrust of hurricane force wind at the defenceless body of the pilot, stripping the remote control from his hands and sending it cartwheeling across the ground.

Realising the Garden was about to turn violent and ugly, the unknown poet and Wongo turned to run—straight into the large welcoming arm doors of the Fridge. The unknown poet needn't have worried about the Fridge and the shooter that was now sticking into his ribs. It was the rotors of the unmanned Japanese manufactured pilotless drone now spinning out of control and travelling at full speed towards his jugular on a kamikaze aircraft mission that would do for him.

The splattering of unknown poet blood went all over the expensive whistle of the Fridge—the unknown poet began dying a horrible convulsive death. Under the circumstances this was the best possible death he could have hoped for and should have felt lucky by it.

The last thing Mr Wongo saw before dying was the victorious pterodactyl that had successfully crash-landed into the turkey oak and was now roosting happily, having defeated the drone enemy—it was just waiting for his poetic words that would never come.

Wongo was looking up at the Fridge with his best cute face like he was his newly adopted owner. The Fridge knew that he should walk Wongo back to the mota and the roasting death that he so richly deserved. He couldn't do it. He pointed his current bun at Wongo's head to despatch him painlessly—Wongo licked the current bun.

# MOOM MONSTERS (V)

Anyway, nobody knew exactly where the Wily-Wily came from. It didn't come from the sky like a normal wind. Maybe we will discover where it came from and learn more about the evil family in other times of bed? The Wily-Wily was fast and furious; like a hurricane in a bad mood, travelling at over 200 miles per hour! It was not just the speed of the Wily-Wily that made it different—the Wily-Wily was luminous—you could actually see it! It was coloured pink, green, yellow, blue and violet. It was a multi-coloured wind, at once the most beautiful and the most dangerous thing you can imagine. It would blow away a city as easy as you would blow the seeds from a dandelion flower. What was even more amazing about the Wily-Wily was that it always arrived at night, and it always arrived the evening after the Moom Monsters!

You see, Freddie, without the Moom Monsters the city of Murria and its people would not exist. The Wily-Wily would sweep them into the ocean, destroying their homes, ships, crops, orchards and livestock. The great civilisation of the Mu would disappear forever. You recollect me comparing the Moom with an Oyster?

After their long journey and sleep, the Moom were ravenously hungry. The Moom didn't take breakfast. The Moom were night eaters. Take the size of your sleepover midnight feasts and multiply them by the biggest number you can think of. That will give you a good idea of the amount of grub they could gobble down. The Moom took their seats at the dining table of the escarpment leading down to the Valley of the Mu and the City of Murria below. Their food was on its way.

The terrifying wind with the shout of a giant thundered beautifully in from the East. Hold on to your bed, Freddie, the Wily-Wily is coming! The great lighthouses and harbour walls gritted their stone teeth and like the ancient marvels of engineering they were, they stood their ground. The Wily-Wily wanted to get its destructive teeth into something; it was a hunting wind. Funnelled into the bay, it hit landfall, roaring across the rocky shore and up and over the cliffs towards the City of Murria. To the Moom the sound of the Wily-Wily was no more than the sound of the dinner bell ringing. The Moom Monsters loved the Wily-Wily. Without the Wily-Wily they would not exist. The Moom opened their giant mouths wide as if they were at the dentist. Not that they have teeth: it would take them weeks to clean them once a day never mind twice! Food was served! The Moom was the predator and the Wily-Wily the prey! They hoovered up the coloured wind like you hoover up Easter eggs! It was a bit blustery down below in the City of Murria where some Wily-Wily crumbs had missed the mouths of the Moom but nothing to worry about. You don't grow to be as big as a Moom without having a healthy appetite. The Moom gorged on the wind all night, they licked their plates of wind and had seconds and thirds and on and on until it had eaten all that the wind waiter had to bring, when daybreak arrived. Then, like your dad after his Christmas dinner, they fell asleep but without wearing a silly hat and jumper! Now you know why the Mu was so pleased to see the Moom Monsters coming and the reason some Mu folk referred to them as the Wily Wily.

The Magno Vento Comedenti had truly lived up to the meaning of its latin name: Great Wind Eater!

The oyster? Well, the Wily-Wily wind was like a grain of sand. Instead of turning the wind into a pearl the Moom Monsters turned it into Glowing Gold! Like gold, but even more precious. The Mooms' glowing belly of gold was made from the Wily-Wily Wind.

It must be time to mention poo. Have I mentioned poo yet? No I didn't think so. No bedtime story worth its salt is complete without it. The valley of the Mu was renowned for its fertility. Murria was the fruit and vegetable capital of the ancient world. Everything flourished. You should have seen the size of their turnips! What was the secret of this horticultural success? Moom poo.

The Mu harvested the poo. Whilst the Mooms' enormous mouths faced east to eat the Wily-Wily the Mooms' bottoms faced west. Moom poo would slide down the steep hill like an avalanche to the bottom of the valley where the Mu farmers waited with their pitchforks and spades to shovel it into their carts. It was a very efficient conveyor belt operation. The Mu would then distribute the poo to their stores, factories, farms, orchards, and vineyards. Chateau Moomchild was the most coveted and sought after bottle of wine ever made, described as an 'immortal superstar of a wine'. Its secret ingredient? You guessed it. Who put the poo in shampoo? It was the Mu that put the poo in shampoo!

In the summer the fruitful valley hummed with rich lushness. Flowers were wild with colour casting their fragrance on the breeze; fat bumblebees bumbled with extra bumbleness—is there any better sound than a bumblebee? The butterflies fluttered and birds sang in the fizzingly happy atmosphere. Sadly, the taste of Murria Honey has now been lost to our taste buds, but there were legends of it being the most delicious food known to the tongue.

Moom poo was very versatile. Not only did it make a great fertiliser to grow food, it was also used to build the entire city's magnificent buildings. The beautiful city of Murria was also known as the Pink City. Moom poo was pale pink. The Pink colour of the Wily-Wily food was a bit like sweet corn, being very hard to digest!

The people of Murria never thought about the glowing gold inside the belly of the Moom. The Moom's value to their lives went far beyond material wealth and greed. Not everybody was as wise as the Mu though, Freddie, but that is for another time of bed story.

I know you can't get enough of them but there are just two more important Moom poo facts that need to be told. The first is that Moom poo did not pong. It didn't smell, it was completely odourless; the second is that you could actually eat it! The Mu had an ancient saying: "A piece of Moom poo a day keeps the doctor away!" Moom poo had great medicinal properties, which is one of the reasons the Mu lived to a good age. What did it taste like? Well, nobody really knows. We do know it was pink so maybe it tasted of Turkish delight, pink jelly or even pink custard? One thing is for sure—it tasted of Moom poo.

# WEAPONISATION

We are go for launch! Main engine start! Cabin doors to automatic! Lift-off! We have a lift-off!

BOOM!

The powder keg that was Cheltenhamshire erupted. The Guantanamo Liberation Army's public service announcements & text messages detonated Krakatoa. It was just the long overdue call to action the oppressed citizens of Cheltenhamshire had been waiting for, and what the police had always feared and so meticulously planned for.

They planned for the worst.

It was worse than the worst.

This was never going to be a non-violent, gentle revolution.

To paraphrase the anthem of a well-known football club whose fans would have loved to have been in the vanguard of such a noble, violent insurrection: *Let 'em come, Let 'em come, Let 'em come, Let 'em all come down to The Square.*

They did come.

They came in great numbers.

The Krakatoan Open uprising tournament was open to all-comers over the age of 17 with at least two years driving or pedestrian experience, regardless of race, colour or creed.

Old folks exited old folks' homes and lodges by any means they could, grabbing anything that looked remotely lethal. They wouldn't have been in these places so prematurely if it wasn't for the toll Guantanamo had taken on their lives in the first place. Hospital patients discharged themselves from hospital; the vast majority of their illnesses were directly attributable to Guantanamo. If you'd lived in this town and held a driving licence for more than two years the chances were you were on your way to Wellington Square.

A local lorry driver, who'd clocked up a thousand lifetimes of pain at Guantanamo's abusive hands, had finally been released from its gravitational field. The radio message was like religious music to him. He drove his lorry straight through Becher's Brook like it was a border checkpoint to freedom and into the Garden with a full cargo of garden tools.

The resistance driver opened the large shutter doors, climbed inside and shouted loudly, "GET YOUR GARDEN TOOLS!" like he was some guerrilla market trader in gardening equipment.

Business was brisk; immediately there was an unorderly queue of people impatiently wanting these munitions. The driver handed them out like a medieval armourer from the Tower of London: pruning shears, spades, forks of all sizes, rakes, hedge shears, axes, hoes and loppers. It's not long ago that this stuff was considered state of the art warfare weaponry.

# BODY BAGS

Outsiders couldn't understand why the Town had gone crazy. That's why they dialled the emergency services.

Here is an extract from one of the early, less hysterical callers:

"Hello, emergency service operator, which service do you require: fire, police, or ambulance?

"Police or better still the Army!"

"I'll just connect you now."

"Hello, where are you calling from?"

"Wellington Square."

"What is the nature?"

"Come quick, there is a riot in Wellington Square— bring body bags—lots of them, and firearms!" Hangs up.

"Hello, emergency service operator, which service do you require: fire, police, or ambulance?"

"Police."

"I'll just connect you now."

"Hello, where are you calling from?"

"It's me again—you'll need pump action shotguns, submachine guns, water cannon, CS gas and as much ammunition as you can carry! Tell my wife and kids I love them."

# CASUALTIES

Dastardly and Mutley had eaten Victor Hugo. Victor had long ago forgotten how to fly. Flight was lost to him now. He loved the shoulder of his owner more than the sky. They'd never tasted parrot before but it made a welcome dietary supplement from human fingers. Macaw Man and Moira had been swept up by the broom wagon of events.

The lorry was on fire. Some of the old folks brought matches. Four retired Morris Men from the Cotswold Chapter were causing carnage with accurate heavy blows from their sticks. The hourglass and the podophile lay unconscious on the grass. Morris men are a nasty bunch; they will render a woman unconscious without a second thought, especially one that looks remotely like a Highways and Parking worker.

Lying unconscious on the battlefield was just the beginning of their problems. A birder who went by the name of Speckle had gone berserk under the trauma of the battle—you have to have sympathy for the lad. He'd fallen upon the hourglass, ripping her blouse and bra off to reveal a fantastic pair of recently enhanced knockers. Speckle didn't want to die a virgin and who could blame him. Kneeling between her legs he hurriedly unbuttoned his skinny jeans and pulled them down, along with his bird patterned boxers. Before he could enjoy his rightful spoils of war, two elderly women plunged knitting needles into his back. For the moment, the hourglasses breasts were safe.

A well-upholstered nurse from the local hospital put her ear to the mouth of the podophile to check he was still breathing. Much to her great relief and delight, he was. By the time she got to the mobile weapons store it was empty and on fire, resulting in her being unarmed and therefore badly handicapped for any battle. Unperturbed, she creatively sat on the podophile with her enormous buttocks and began suffocating him to death. A man with an axe chopped off the podophile's feet to stop him running away and to make sure he got the good suffocating he deserved.

The beautiful exposed breasts of the hourglass not surprisingly caught the attention of a man with a pair of large loppers. Loppers and breasts don't mix. It was just the sort of thing he'd been looking to lop off since he entered the square, mad as hell. "Highways scum," said the nurse still sitting on her dead husband, looking in the direction of his wife.

Lop, lop went the loppers.

The Knitting Needle Two began lustily taking Speckle's virginity—it was not what he would have wanted but fortunately for him he was dead!

# WONGO THE WONDER DOG (III)

Wongo had been defrosting the Fridge, a cold-blooded murderer. For twenty minutes the Fridge had been standing pointing the gun at Wongo, tears streaming down his chubby cheeks, unable to pull the trigger whilst the battle raged all around them.

Folks in these parts weren't going to stand by and let a man hold a gun to an innocent creature's head for that long.

A unisex army of medieval troops holding pitchforks like trident spears surrounded the Fridge. To give the killer his professional due he didn't go down without a fight. His father—the Tumbledryer—would want to know that. He gave Wongo a fond tender farewell stroke on his empty head before letting him off the lead and shooing him to run off like a cowboy sending his faithful horse back home now he'd reached the end of the road.

By the time the first javelin pitchfork had pierced his body the Fridge had managed to get away four good bullets of death. Some of the soldiers were a little rusty with their throwing accuracy, with a good many becoming the blameless victims of collateral damage. The Fridge's temperature fell dramatically as the blood ran from multiple puncture wounds. From space he would look like a giant pincushion. Tridents bounced out of the treble twenty that was the Fridge's body as there was no room in the bed. There are only so many pitchforks that can fit into the border of one man's body.

# THE SOUND OF MUSIC

The square was alive to the sound of music. The alphorn player hadn't stopped since the battle of Wellington Square began. He was like the piper, the trumpeter or drummer boy. He'd been standing, puffing on the giant pipe like a one-man military brass band on the Titanic. It was like the alphorn was calling the people to an evening prayer of killing.

It was the first time he'd played his alphorn outside of his native Switzerland. This was also a premier for Wellington Square. Never before in its over 200-year history had it listened to the sound of the alphorn. The first notes went out eagerly in search of the high mountain with its thinning air. The labrophone dials up to connect with eternal place and time before redirecting it to dissolve in the hearts and memories of the listeners. It was the voice of the past, present and future.

No signal. Sorry we are unable to connect you. That's what the Garden Square said to the music. The alphornist was sending the notes to their deaths in the heavy, foreign Cotswold air. Suffering from fatal homesickness, they dropped to the earth like vibrating sycamore seeds, falling with terminal melancholy upon the grass, the living, the soon to be dead, dead, and the dying.

The sound of dying notes was deeply soothing to the human ear.

Every year the celebrity alphornist would return to Wellington Square for an all expenses paid remembrance ceremony. Dignitaries would place wreaths at the feet of the shrine of The Lady of Cheltenhamshire. You could feel the happiness of the spirits of the happy dead. The same alphorn would blow out like the last post, connecting with eternal place and time, redirecting it to dissolve in the hearts and memories of the listeners. It was the voice of the past, present and future.

# WHADDNEY THE ROBIN (II)

With the Dutch courage of five pints of lager swilling around in his red belly, Whaddney had bravely bob-bob-bobbin'd into the square. The time to "live, love, laugh and be happy" was almost up.

If ever the Robin needed Batman this was it. Even the caped crusader would have struggled to survive for five minutes in this hell, even with the benefit of a few beverages. He quickly came across the young desecrated body of Speckle—if Batman had been alongside him he would have surely uttered, "Holy knit one pearl two." If he'd had known what ensued—"Holy fate worse-than-death!" Instead, Robin just said, 'Holy Shit!'

A lot of terminally ill humans came to the Garden to die legally and with dignity.

A dying woman wearing just a hospital gown and wristband and pushing her drip had shuffled up to Whaddney. She wasn't going to be fooled by the Highways & Parking worker's disguise. Whaddney could smell eau de death upon her. Her skin was RAL9010—Death Light Grey—the preferred colour of the dying. She couldn't see Whaddney smiling with compassion beneath his costume. It wouldn't have made any difference. From behind her back, with the last throes of her life, she thrust a stolen scalpel straight into the robin redbreast of Whaddney. His breast grew a darker and darker red. It was the last gallant act of her long life—she fell to her old knees—the sight of Whaddney keeling over backwards was more beautiful than the morphine that had been killing the pain inside of her. She died blissfully happy in the certain knowledge that she had done her bit in the war against Guantanamo. What a way to go.

# GARDENERS' WORLD

It's been easy pickings for the two traffic wardens patrolling the square for the last few days. For some reason, they hunted in male and female pairs. For the most part, with the exception of half a dozen professional looking Nazi salutes directed at them, it had been business as usual. Both were diminutive but they felt ten feet tall in their Hugo Boss uniforms made of fear fabric. The multiple red stripes on their armbands told you they had countless ticketing kills to their names. Their computer and ticket machines hung like holsters; these two sheriffs were quick on the penalty notice draw. These Civil Enforcement Officers had their work cut out because there was a lot of civil enforcing to be done; they were going to need a bigger posse. They'd been on their two-way radios pleading for back up. Nobody had got his or her back. These unarmed foot soldiers were on the front line of Gittler's war on the public. They were always going to be dead meat cannon fodder when Krakatoa erupted.

Well-organised bands of Krakatoans were actually using the spades and shovels for their intended purpose. They'd dug two very large holes and buried the traffic wardens up to their necks facing each other. They had it coming. Like good horticulturists they made sure to tuck the soil in nice and tightly just above their shoulders to make sure there were no air pockets. They gave them a good healthy nitrogen-phosphorus-potassium based urine fertilizer to help get them established. It was like a macabre episode of Gardeners' World.

The gardeners thoughtfully replaced their black hats to help identify their plants. They held their garden instruments aloft chanting, "DEATH! DEATH! DEATH!" Judging by the look on the plants' faces this wasn't the kind of talking-to-plants conversation that was going to improve their health. Now would have been a good time to offer up a prayer to the patron saint of traffic wardens. Squabbles quickly broke out between the Loppers and the Axes as to who was best equipped to dead head them. Parking & Ticket began reminiscing to each other:

"Do you remember when we ticketed that entire funeral cortege containing those mourning families and friends?"

"I will never forget it, it was one of the happiest days of my life."

"What about the time we ticketed that woman for pulling over to help resuscitate a heart attack victim lying in the middle of the road?"

"Don't forget the lady who purchased a parking ticket just as her waters broke. The priceless look on her face as she shuffled uncomfortably towards me, waving her ticket in the air, soaking—it just gave me enough time to finish writing out her ticket. Sorry luv, already written," he said, laughing loudly.

"We've had some good times together, haven't we?"

"The best days of my life."

"I love you."

"I—"

A bloke driving a mobility scooter quickly settled the decapitation argument. The scooter looked more like a retro motorcycle from the *Easy Rider* movie with its chrome bumper, mudguards, handlebars, and suspension, complete with spoke wheels. Mobility scooter numbers had been steadily growing, with at least a dozen wreaking havoc like demented dodgem cars in the enclosure of the fun fair of Wellington Square.

The driver was listening to his favourite tracks on full volume through large headphones. His scooter has been pimped with a large antenna covered in patriotic flags. The 'Modfather' wore an open faced touring helmet with visor and R.A.F logo, which he'd matched with a vintage mod fishtail parka jacket in combat green that he'd covered in embroidered and enamel badges; he was as keen as mod mustard to join in the killing.

He couldn't believe his luck when he saw the two traffic wardens' heads asking to be severed. This was going to be a high point in mobility scooter history. The expensive restoration work that took place following the battle was worth every penny after it set a world record mobility scooter price at Christie's 'Wellington Square Memorabilia Auction.' The ill-fated blood stained traffic warden hats sold as a pair to a wealthy overseas telephone buyer for a cool 10 million. It was a scandal to see such great historical artefacts and national treasures leave the shores of this great nation.

The scooter's maximum speed of 8 mph combined with its 30 stone ballast did a half decent job of semi-decapitation before throwing the Mod from the scooter. The gardeners enthusiastically moved in to finish off Parking & Ticket as well as smiting the Mod into chum for good measure. The final word he heard in his life through his headphones was "yeah!"

"In this town called Malice, ooh yeah!"

# 100% TOLERANCE

That's what the good people of Cheltenhamshire had. One hundred percent tolerance for killing. Guantanamo for years had been programming the people of Cheltenhamshire like an evil mesmerist. Krakatoa was simply the click of the fingers that unleashed their bottled up rage, turning citizens into happy homicidal maniacs.

The killing is good—for the killing was purifying the people of all their anger, stress and unfulfilled dreams and expectations, liberating them from yet another day weighed down by the falsehoods and disappointments of life.

A lot of people needed purifying.

Wellington Square was a purification factory; it was the purification capital of the world. People were queuing up to be purified. The factory couldn't keep up with the demand for its goods.

The killing is good. The killing *is* good.

Quite rightly, Guantanamo was largely to blame for it all.

Initially, butchering a fascist from the Highways & Parking department provided the ultimate purification for the soul. Money couldn't buy you a better first class unburdening. Sadly, there weren't enough fascists to go around.

The Krakatoans needed purging badly.

There was no turning away mass hysteria unsatisfied. The factory was happy to accept second-class indiscriminate slaying if it helped.

It did.

A beautiful bloodlust was setting them free, giving meaning to their lives for the very first time.

They needed to enjoy it whilst it lasted.

Cheltenhamshire would be a kinder, more compassionate place for it once this was over. Patience and tolerance would replace the suffering.

Everyone was going to feel better once the killing was done—even the dead. The killing is good, feels good.

# BUBBLES

Bubbles' lover, like so many, was at the edge of death; he wouldn't be turning back to life. He'd received a mortal blow to the head with the steering wheel of a Nissan Micra. Nasty. In a show of defiance and solidarity, a lot of liberators brought with them their steering wheels, many more their number plates; they'd endured a lot together: their vehicles were just as much an innocent victim as they were—they wanted them to witness the victory over their tormentors, share with them the sweet satisfaction of justice.

Many people understandably lost their grip on sanity during the battle, including a large man with a loud bass voice who stood nearby the stricken Mr Bubbles shouting 'STOP BREXIT!' repeatedly. His brain was now the equivalent of a robot whose computer chips had been so badly damaged that no matter what buttons you pressed he was now stuck with two words for the rest of his life.

Mr Bubbles heroically tried to command Bubbles to return home away from the danger. Bubbles may have done so if it weren't for Wongo arriving on the scene after he'd picked up Bubbles' fragrant scent wafting into his nostrils. You can't keep a good dog down. Wongo had always fancied Bubbles, with her flowing silky locks and shapely figure. She could advertise shampoo and conditioner. It was turning out to be a great day out for Wongo and this could be the icing on the cake. Bubbles had always wanted a bit of rough and Wongo fitted that bill perfectly. She'd never had sex with another dog before, only her human lover.

Wongo and Bubbles got it on right in front of Bubbles' stricken owner. Bubbles howled with pleasure.

Mr Bubbles deserved better.

What a slut.

'STOP BREXIT!'

# G-DAY

It was incredible how the community pulled together following Krakatoa's eruption. The humanity of people brought tears to your eyes. The people of Cheltenhamshire could rightly be proud of their behaviour. The local clergy—imams, rabbis, ministers, monks and nuns—had all been quick to praise their actions as the will of God. Many set an example to their followers by joining in the massacre.

Cobblers Corner had become the de facto nerve centre of the Krakatoans due to its strategic geographical location on the main artery of Guantanamo—pointing directly in the direction of Wellington Square. Tap and Stitch reopened the shop. Tap busily handed out cobbler's lasts, anvils, awls, hammers, knives, mallets and scissors, anything that might inflict a mortal injury on a Highways & Parking official. Stitch was doing a grand job directing operations with a large, loud hailer like he was the beachmaster during the D-Day Normandy landings.

A 100-year-old WWII veteran of Sword Beach, proudly wearing his Green Beret and war medals including the Legion of Honour, passed him, being pushed in a wheelchair by his proud father. Reginald or Reg as he was known, was one of the few ex-servicemen that actually enjoyed talking about the war and in particular revelling in the number of Nazis he'd killed. With his steely war game face on, Reg had no intention of returning from Wellington Square alive. He'd carried 80 years of guilt for surviving his comrades and friends. A later citation from the Battle recommended Reg received a posthumous medal for gallantry. It went on to record his last known heroic words: "DIE, YOU FASCIST BASTARDS!"

"It's on foot from here on in, mate, you'll have to abandon it with the other vehicles," said Stitch to a chap driving a vintage steamroller and simultaneously ending his long-held dream of flattening a human with it. The steamroller was abandoned next to a white van with a giant wooden rat perched on top of it. 'Rob the Rat,' to his friends, aka the 'verminator,' had donned the full bee-keeping garb and poison thrower vermin busting back pack and beetled off bravely to do his duty. Brings a lump to your throat. "When I sticks this in mind they'll be fucking livid!" he said cheerfully to Stitch in passing. Tragically for 'Rob the Rat' he would die like Mij the otter in the film Ring of Bright Water with a blow to the back of the head with a heavy spade.

Cheltshireons were leaning out of windows, cheering and shouting encouragement—"Kill one for me!" It was as if the British Army had liberated them. This was G-Day—Guantanamo was falling.

When the Krakatoans finally reached their destination they weren't disappointed with how well organised the slaughter had become. It was like a pleasure fun fair square of death. The Brits are good at organising events on this scale and it showed.

Volunteers wearing high visibility jackets were positioned at each gate as well as the large gap made by the hero HGV arms driver in Becher's Brook. They were sat in folding camping chairs with cups of tea and coffee in the arms of the drink holders. Some were waving Union

Jacks patriotically. These were the very same people you would see giving up their time verifying your name in polling booths during elections. It's like they had volunteered to be marshals at the Olympic games of killing. The queue was now full of a lot of happy sombrero-wearing Condor fans.

# EMERGENCY SERVICES

Where the hell are the emergency services? Where's the Army? What happened to Operation Krakatoa? These questions demanded an answer.

"This is not a drill." That was what it said on the authentication orders to commence Operation Krakatoa. Our public service heroes had sworn oaths to protect the people and by God they were going to do their duty!

Everything had gone perfectly to plan. Help was not on its way. Help had been stood down. The last thing these people needed was help. They would never be forgiven for interfering in the natural justice that they all so richly deserved. They fully sympathised and supported the just cause of the Krakatoans. Many of their off-duty colleagues were already on their way to join in the celebration of life that is the Good Killing.

Negotiating with the people would be futile; they would be sending uniformed officers to their certain death.

The chiefs of the emergency services patted themselves on the back with smug satisfaction at its complete success. All those hours of practice had paid off. They would just sit tight now and let Krakatoa blow itself out.

# BAD DAY AT WELLINGTON SQUARE

The newly formed Cheltenhamshire Mounted Police Team was still in its infancy with only two horses on loan from the Metropolitan Police. That's the reason they didn't get the call to stand down—they'd been forgotten.

You can bet your bottom dollar that the wily Met weren't sending the yokels of Cheltenhamshire their finest animal recruits. The greys—Boris and Livingstone—were close to being put out to pasture with no ambition left other than retirement. Up to now they had enjoyed their trips to local schools and being lovingly patted by drunken people.

Their volunteer riders—'The Magnificent Two'—were not magnificent. The careers of police officers 'Calamity' Jane, and John the 'Duke' Wayne, as their colleagues had quickly christened them, had hit rock bottom. Volunteering was their last chance saloon attempt to revive their careers. The brains were definitely not holding the reins.

What looked to be a routine Saturday evening for Boris and Livingstone had now taken a dramatic twist. Our cowgirl and cowboy had been given the rogue order to scramble from their camouflaged stable, saddle up and giddy-up over to Welly.

Boris and Livingstone bolted out of their stables at walking pace, completely ignoring the urgings of their marshals to break into a trot.

Our gunslingers were not exactly slinging guns. They

were not tooled up to bring in the wild and mean outlaws of the West that were the Krakatoan gang:

"Stick 'em up!"

"Or what?"

"We'll fill ya full of PVA spray."

At least they could give a Stetson nod to the past with the handcuffs they were carrying.

Calamity and The Duke couldn't believe the scene of carnage and lovely Krakatoan lawlessness that eventually greeted them. 'Bad Day at Wellington Square' would have been a suitably understated title for this western movie. It was a sell out riot. The Garden coliseum was at full capacity—there must have been 20 thousand people in the stadium and many more were queuing to get in. The Krakatoans couldn't kill each other quick enough. Boris and Livingstone—veterans of many a riot—instantly grasped the jeopardy of the situation, simultaneously depositing two large pyramids of horse manure before turning quickly to retreat. They appraised the situation rather more quickly than their stunned passengers.

"I'm requisitioning this horse in the name of Guantanamo," said a man dressed as a Red Indian covered in blood.

"In the name of Guantanamo," repeated a member of the horse rustling gang.

Boris didn't know it yet but his career had just taken a turn for the better. Future generations would speak his name in the same breathe as Bucephalus, the horse of Alexander the Great. A bronze statue would be unveiled of him rearing up majestically in the middle of a new town centre roundabout.

Brady and his bunch of followers allowed Livingstone

to return to the stables, carrying with him the handcuffed Magnificent Two: 'Dum, dum da-dum, da da da da da dum...'

# TIME OF DEATH

7<sup>th</sup> October 2018, at 6.30pm and 7 seconds. The sky had clouded over to cover its eyes from the events below. It was two minutes before the sun set. The moon was in Taurus. The Man of Gloom was dead age 50. The Man of Gloom (MoG): 1968–2018. He'd gloomed about the year that would bookend his life. It was out there waiting for him, stalking him. Not even his most pessimistic glooming predicted today.

The Scared of Dying Society was an instant success. In the space of a few months it had secured over 10 million petrified paid-up subscribers and growing. The website was an unexpected money making machine. These people would do anything to find the elixir of life everlasting, and there were plenty of folk out there who could offer it to them at the right price!

MoG didn't kill anyone before dying so his soul had not been purified. Earlier on in the day he'd had a flu jab at the local pharmacy so at least he wouldn't get flu in the afterlife he'd planned for.

MoG had just signed a lucrative deal with the CRYONIC CORPORATION to advertise on his website, which included him negotiating a free space in one of their expensive liquid nitrogen embalming freezers—Iceland for the dead. At some point in the future he would be defrosted back to life to resume his fear of a second death. All Cryonic needed was his body.

The Man of Gloom was the last person to die in the

square.

The consolation of this fact was lost to him.

He ran into the Garden fearing death once more.

Death came to him in the form of a banjo.

It was a five-string banjo.

Only the night before the duelling banjo had been playing traditional folk and bluegrass music. The last song it ever played was: 'For the Widows in Paradise, For the Fatherless in Ypsilanti.'

It would have been a good way for the banjo to bow out if it didn't have to listen to the banjoist murdering the ballad with his singing.

The banjo player took the banjo to the Man of Gloom's head like he was Pete Townshend and his head was the stage. Dazed and incapacitated MoG was a sitting death duck. He was strangled by the banjo's nickel C string. For good measure, the banjo player kicked the corpse like it was a speaker. This dying was not among his countless joyless ruminations on how he might pop his clogs. It was grim even by Grim Reaper standards.

The banjo player would sadly survive to write a folk song in memory of his old banjo and the sacrifice it made in liberating Guantanamo. His new banjo would always feel uncomfortable playing it, let alone listening to it:

*There's an achin' in my knee*
*Where my banjo used to be*
*It died to set us free*
*Donatin' its string in C*

*It'll be strummin' an pickin' in heaven*
*It'll be strummin' an pickin' in heaven...*

Cryonically, the Man of Gloom's body was now in breach of the Cryonic Corpse-orations terms and conditions owing to the fact the body was incomplete. Incomplete was an understatement. If his body were a 1000 piece jigsaw puzzle, 999 pieces were missing. All the king's horse and all the king's men couldn't put Gloomy back together again! The Man of Gloom would just have to take his life after death chances like everyone else.

The people of Cheltenhamshire had shown some inventive ways to kill each other. There had been a lot of bludgeoning. Bludgeoning had led the way. The American baseball bat had usurped the native rounder bat as the most popular bludgeon of choice. For a minority sport there were an awful lot of baseball players in Cheltenhamshire. It did warm your heart to hear the traditional English chant of "ROUNDER! ROUNDER! ROUNDER!" as a female rounder team battered to death a suspected Chancellery cleaning lady. Many people had been bludgeoned to death with everyday instruments of death. Survivors are to this day still cooking up the full English with their non-stick frying pans; sausages sizzle with added sizzling at the honour.

Impact resistant ten pin bowling balls automatically make their way back to the hands of their owners, now proudly bearing an active service inscription.

Cricket bats have returned to the more familiar sound of leather on willow.

Killer heels have given up their killing and returned to stilettos.

The last surviving fascist member of Gittler's High Command proved what a total scumbag he was when trying to save his own reptilian skin by desperately lashing out in self-defence with the stolen iron of a dead woman. What kind of savages were these people? Only a few hours before she had been lovingly ironing her husband's cotton shirts for work whilst listening to the radio when she received the call to arms.

Fortunately, as every iron lobbyist knows, the only way to stop a bad guy with an iron is with a good guy with an iron.

Steaming with anger, Iron Man came to the rescue. Rotating it above his head like a hammer thrower wielding a gladiatorial morning star on a three-pin plug chain, the clothes iron flew at great velocity into the fascist's forehead. He fell like Goliath.

Like Goliath, he lost his head. The topiarists brought with them their chainsaws. The sound of the chainsaw birds filled the Garden air. They found it wasn't easy to shape a human into a peacock or poodle, so they kept it simple, dismembering the dead and the dying like they were a lumberjack and the bodies were the logs.

# PERVERT'S PARADISE

It would have been impossible to move around the Garden for corpses if it wasn't for the commendable hygienic work of the gardeners keeping everything in order. These unsung groundsmen and groundswomen heroes had done a terrific job of the back-breaking work of chopping up the dead bodies into small pieces and shovelling them into funeral pyres for the burning squads to burn them.

Some bodies were taken by Cheltenhamshire's small but highly active cannibal population, eaten before they could get to them. The Bishop of Cheltenhamshire, wearing her black and red cassock and mitre, was one such high profile victim. Cannibals have a long history of devouring their favourite food—missionaries. The Bishop wasn't going to be eaten without a fight. Her crosier and fighting staff already had a number of God's kills to her name on this noble crusade for justice, guaranteeing her martyrdom.

The cannibals circled the Right Reverend Bishop Joan like a pack of mouth-watering hyenas. One hyena went for her ankles. That was a mistake. Joan liked her shapely ankles and smote the ankle dog from this life, snapping her crosier as she did so on his skull. Surrounded and defenceless, she fell to her knees and offered up a last final prayer to her assailants:

"For what you are about to eat may the Lord make you truly thankful."

Amen.

Many people found the battle body parts highly erotic. The fetishists fought hard to remain, giving nose, ear, elbow and various other kinds of bodily lingus—still sucking like leeches they were pulled squelching from the corpses.

These people are amongst us.

Perverts are amongst us—in great numbers.

The Square was a pervert's paradise.

A middle-aged woman masqueraded as a paramedic, wearing a green uniform and carrying a large medical backpack. Her pack was packed full of homemade English mustard & very hot horseradish sauce. She just wanted to share her food fetish addiction for brainfire—the opposite of brainfreeze. Other people shouldn't be denied the exquisite pleasure she found so arousing. She tilted back the heads of the wounded and spoon-fed them the fiery condiments, holding their mouths and noses shut whilst watching the confused facial contortions the shock produced. "That will make you feel better," she said before snorting a well-earned line of horseradish herself and moving onto the next dying diner.

Miss Brainfire didn't have the sole food fetish rights to the Battle of Wellington Square. Mr Chilli was busily administering the 'Carolina Reaper' pepper, one of the hottest peppers in the world, with a heat 200 times hotter than a jalapeno. He sprinkled the chilli pods liberally into eyes, open wounds and mouths at every opportunity. Mr Chilli bumped into Miss Brainfire, who'd fallen victim to a young man who'd been revived by some of her English mustard enough to re-join the fray and reward her with a good kicking to death. She looked up at Mr Chilli with one last gasping, dying request:

"Horseradish," she wheezed.

"You got it," said Mr Chilli, administering the reaper last rights.

Mr Chilli's chilli campaign finally got the ending it warranted. A resident of Welly, a fine looking man of unimpeachable character, who must remain nameless for legal reasons, was returning home having nipped out on a vital mission to the local stores to stock up on his blossoming pregnant wife's favourite food craving, when he got willingly sucked into the hypnotic Good Killing. He wanted his unborn child to be proud of his father.

Mr Unimpeachable came across Mr Chilli, who by now was nearly out of chilli ammo, cradling the head of another Krakatoan goner.

"Water, water," croaked the goner.

"Sure, sure," said Mr Chilli, preparing his final sachet of fire.

Mr Chilli didn't know what had hit him from this world to the great chilli pepper in the sky. Unimpeachable stoved his head with a large tin of pickled gherkins and in doing so got himself on the purification killer board early doors. Just peachy. His child would be proud. There would be hell on when he returned home late to his pickled gherkin-craving wife.

The gardeners suffered heavy casualties; being an orderly during the battle left them vulnerable and defenceless. One young gardener lay dying when one of his comrades reassuringly loomed over him carrying his spade. "Chop me up good, bro," was his dying wish. The brother mercifully granted his last request to the letter.

I LOVE WHEELBARROW was head over wheels in love with wheelbarrow. Besotted. He'd demonstrated his love for wheelbarrow by bringing wheelbarrow to the demonstration. They were inseparable. He put the love of his life to good work by transporting the liberated dead to the bonfires. In those moments he'd never loved his wheelbarrow so much. Exhausted, he collapsed into the barrow bower bed of her belly and slept the happiest sleep of his life.

Daddy Long Legs just wouldn't die. No matter what the Krakatoans threw at him he kept coming back to annoying, erratic life. He was now down to just two legs. Death by Daddy Long Legs was a terrifying nightmare for many people. Their terror was fully justified. The Daddy would hover above the dying like a spectre of death arriving to collect them. He then clumsily touched their faces repeatedly with his long legs. "Looks like another taken by the Daddy," said one of the body burners, noticing the facial constriction of horrified fear on the corpse.

Paul had arrived in the Garden in search of his son Peter.

Paul carried with him his large anger.

The purification factory wanted his anger.

Paul was a killing ace.

The Garden was a priest.

Paul's sins were well and truly behind him now thanks to the absolution. Peter and Paul were reunited in an autumn mist that could have blown in from the land of Honah Lee. They hugged—slowly squeezing the life and love back into each other.

# AVALON

At 6.36pm and 8 seconds Brady brought the square to killing-free silence—with the exception of the ever-present soothing alphorn. By now the STOP BREXIT madman whose path back to sanity was lost forever was mouthing the words silently instead, like a goldfish.

After the warmth of the day a late afternoon autumnal mist had fallen on the square like the mists of Avalon.

Sitting Bull was an instantly recognisable figure in this town. The crazed people of Cheltenhamshire had a lot of respect for Brady. If anyone could cut through the craziness and get a grip on the situation it was 'Wayward Bob,' magnificently sat astride Boris.

Brady could ride, because Brady thought he could ride.

He was crazier than Crazy Horse.

Most people now had at least one Good Killing to their name and were feeling good about life again. There was an equal proportion of female to male corpses—Laughing Bear had made sure of that. He'd enjoyed strangling a lot of women with his bare hands, including a pair of Siamese twins, which tested his strangling skills to the full. Their sacrifice was not in vain, it was a good purging, and just what 'Chalk' needed to get his life back on its natural heterosexual track and make fish Fridays a thing of the past. He now had a newfound respect for women.

Just as the police predicted—Krakatoa had blown itself out. You had to feel sorry for the many thousands of people who would return home having missed out on a once in a lifetime opportunity to receive the purification they so desperately needed and merited.

Donald Trump and Barry the ex Birdman Jones flanked Brady on either side of Boris. Jones, along with a tall man wearing a magnolia Fedora Panama hat and not a scratch on him, were the only birders to survive the battle. God really did hate birders! He owed a great debt of gratitude to the Battle of Wellington Square for setting him free from his birding obsession.

Barry was never going to find the emerald, gold and turquoise birds to fill him with peace. He wasn't going to resurrect Stevie from the dead. When Dusky perished from the gunshot right before his eyes it triggered Barry's unresolved grief:

He let the bereavement in.

It was hazardous stuff.

His mind wasn't ready for the sorrow.

He turned his anger mercilessly on his own people like Darth Vader.

His rare bird pager bleeped in his jacket pocket with news of a rare bearded vulture touching down in Hyde Park. He removed the pager and tossed it into a nearby burning pyre of dead birder bodies like it was the ring returning to Mordor.

Brady brought the mass of now happy freedom fighters behind him to a halt at the foot of the turkey oak before dismounting Boris. The Condor fans were carrying their beloved Whaddney above their sombrero-wearing heads as a mark of respect.

Bob walked up the small grassy knoll covered with shrubs that was the platform and entrance hall of the mighty turkey oak. It marked the final last brave stand of Gittler and his acolytes. Bob never found the identifiable remains of Gittler. He was certainly in no condition to make the front cover of Birdwatching Magazine. With the absence of a body, conspiracy theorists would later speculate that Gittler had escaped to Argentina to start a Second Road Reich. He didn't.

Gittler and his colleagues had quickly formed a protective defensive human wagon wheel around Dusky who was now lying in state. Just being dead wasn't enough for some protestors: they wanted to make it suffer more than that. The higher ground helped them repel the first assault of placard attacks.

Initially, defences held out well, with just a few nasty placard head injuries. Early hand-to-hand combat saw the Highways & Parking team sensibly seize some of the protestors' signs. Within minutes, overwhelming numbers of early Krakatoan responders began to swell the fighting numbers like the Zulus at Rorke's Drift.

The human wagon wheel around the turkey oak began to shrink. Some of Gittler's loyal servants had the intelligence to bite on their suicide cyanide capsules to avoid capture. A ray of hope arrived in the form of twelve loyal traffic wardens rallying to protect their king like the Praetorian Guard. It was a courageous but futile suicide mission. Extinction quickly fell on all the traffic wardens of Cheltenhamshire.

Gittler was now the last highways-scum man standing. He fought on bravely, rendering senseless a heavily pregnant young woman by smashing her over the head with a placard proclaiming FEMINISM MEANS EQUALITY! She just wanted a better future for her unborn child.

That was the last gallant act of Aloysius Gittler's life. A crushing blow to the back of his skull saw him buckle at the knees, his hands fell to his sides and he whirled around as if he were doing a drunken version of the twist. A boxing referee would have stepped into the ring and called off the fight to protect him from further punishment. Further punishment was just what his assailant had dreamt of. She went in for the kill, clubbing him enthusiastically to oblivion with her prosthetic leg whilst hopping on the other. "I'll take it from here," said a man with an axe, selfishly muscling in on all her good clubbing work.

The doctors held Guantanamo directly responsible for the amputation of her leg due to a blood clot caused by the amount of time she was immobile whilst a commuting prisoner. She'd been biding her time ever since.

Bob bent down to pick up a pair of Second World War blood-stained binoculars with broken lenses and returned to his people.

"Guantanamo has fallen!" cried Bob, raising Gittler's binoculars.

The people cheered, deliriously waving their number plates, garden instruments and assorted weapons above their heads like AK47s. They would have fired them jubilantly into the sky if they could. Hugging, kissing and fornication quickly broke out. The PEOPLE AGAINST BUREAUCRACY councillor pumped his placard in the air; this was the kind of free spontaneous society he had campaigned hard for all his life.

The Guantanamo Liberation Army sent out a victory broadcast:

"Comrades, citizens, brothers and sisters; today we give great thanks to almighty God for victory over tyranny, for deliverance from Guantanamo. As an act of thanksgiving let us all get bladdered together."

Although Whaddney was dead, the loyal Condor fans were determined to give him the send-off he deserved. They would take him for a night on the town he would never forget. That evening would live long in the memory. It was as if England had won the World Cup. Cars drove victoriously the wrong way up Guantanamo, beeping their horns and waving Union Jacks and bus lanes were emotionally reunited. The police made their first appearance, allowing the revellers to dance in the town's fountains and letting them wear their helmets, as perfectly scripted by Operation Krakatoa.

The next morning the Home Secretary stood shoulder to shoulder with the Chief of Cheltenhamshire Police and spoke of the deep pride and admiration she felt for the Krakatoans and the brave actions of the Emergency Services. She praised the people of Cheltenhamshire for their restraint and not over-reacting. She would create a new public holiday and national day of celebration in honour of their sacrifice. The new years honours list would be full of ordinary Krakatoan heroes. Bob Brady would later receive a knighthood and Count Flashula was given the flashing freedom of the town.

The celebrations went on into the early hours of the morning. By dawn, the convoy of clear-up teams and their heavy flashing machinery that had been waiting patiently in the wings as part of Operation Krakatoa had returned the square to normal. Even Dusky had been bagged up. All they missed was a single copy of a Collins Bird Watching guide that was poignantly left on the battlefield; its pages blew in the wind as if the wind were reading it. The wind could now tell you a great deal about birds. When the wind filled the wings of the birds it now knew their names.

A long queue of refuse lorries waited patiently to dump its cargo of human remains into the energy waste plant incinerator.

Tut-tut tutted the molecules of Dave.

# THE MACHINE OF HAPPINESS (II)

Bob returned to the relative peace and quiet of his flat. The day's events had been a complete success, beyond his wildest dreams, which was saying something, given the nature of his dreams. All in all it had been a historical day for the WSRC, a job well done. They had killed two birds with one stone, and one of them was a real bird.

They had sacrificed many brave members. Panto Pete had played his last Widow Twankey. 'OH NO HE HASN'T!'

The thunderous thighs of Thunder Thighs had been severed from the rest of her body, Many Husbands had come to the end of the husband road, Window Licker would lick no more—Bob would commission a wooden bench for the Garden with a dedication and their names engraved upon it.

It would be some time before Bob could rent out the machine of happiness.

Happiness in this town was now at record levels.

When eventually his paying customers did turn up they weren't disappointed with the performance of the machine of happiness. They always left smiling, having placed their heads inside a portable barrow cement mixer with an ancient patina of supernatural cement whilst Bob rotated it like a barrel organ. Bob always recommended a minimum of three sessions to get the maximum happiness benefit.

# CROWS

I'm not jealous, but what is it with crows? Shakespeare, Rimbaud, Verlaine, Pessoa, Lorca and many more besides; they all loved penning a crow poem or crow-barring a crow into a poem or verse. You can't be a great poet without one; it's a rite of poet passage and Sir Bob Brady has joined their illustrious ranks with this peach taken from his soon-to-be-published international best selling Wellington Square Manuscripts:

*The hungry Crows devour the evening storm*
*it keeps their feathers dry;*

*a flying black belly of satiated gloom*
*dims the Cheltenhamshire sky.*

*Unseen, a galaxy of Space Crows*
*caw at the stars.*

The crows had returned now the sky has stopped throwing down great cymbals of Black Swan thunder. I've missed them. For crows are the greatest storytellers and raconteurs. You can't beat a shaggy crow story. I am looking forward to telling them about Bob Brady's space crows! They all seem to have a love for my infectious laugh. The more I laugh the more they want to make me laugh more. "Purusa-damya-sarathi," they will say, respecting my status fully. "Did you hear about the scarecrow—" They love scarecrow stories.

# MOVING

Eight months after the great Battle of Wellington Square, a new day, unaware of the living and with nothing better to do, moved into Cheltenhamshire carrying its bronchial valley weather purpose built in forgettable. Happiness radiation had now fallen to the national average. It would take another three years before the stonemasons finished carving the last names of the lucky dead into large stone memorial plinths that would be placed circling the marble statue of Our Lady of Cheltenhamshire.

"Overcast and windy again," said Amelia as she placed a cup of tea gently on Tom's study desk before tenderly resting her head on his shoulder while looking out across the window to the Garden Square.

"Overcast does not do its caster justice," Tom replied before taking a couple of loud slurps of tea to lubricate his mind further.

"It's a masterpiece of murk—if oblivion had a colour you're looking at it!"

"You missed your calling as a TV weather forecaster," said Amelia laughing.

"Our weather is sick now—especially the wind. The wind is the sickest of all —if you could catch it you would section it. It has become a real head-banger; the trees and birds have proclaimed it mad, they don't want anything to do with the wind anymore."

"Pleased to hear the birds and trees confiding in you,"

she said, enjoying the return of his absurd sense of humour. Tom smiled a little awkwardly. The wind conversation triggered a happy memory in Amelia's heart.

"We shall ride out into that grey oblivion," said Tom, recomposing himself doing a bad John Wayne impression and hugging her waist before continuing:

"Let me just finish marking this final piece of English homework."

"You don't know how pleased I am to hear you say that again," said Amelia, affectionately squeezing the knuckle of his hand.

"There is a girl in my class Amelia," said Tom with real excitement in his voice. "Her name is Scarlet Lightning, she lives in the Square; Amelia she is remarkably talented, her work is sublime at just fifteen, publishable."

"She is lucky to have the talented Mr Atkins to nurture her."

"I set them the task of writing a poem, just one line long, and she came up with this; I think you will particularly appreciate it, let me read it to you."

"An ingenious way to keep the marking down, I'm listening."

**The Fastest Spider in the World**
*sprints up & down the cello's fingerboard.*

"I can just picture the crimped horror spider hand of the cellist playing," said Amelia smiling with approval.

"Amelia," said Tom gently, "start playing again." Amelia went silent before replying, "I think I'm ready now to return to the orchestra."

"You don't know how much that means to me, Mrs

Atkins! Speaking of ready, I'm all done," said Tom, smiling warmly.

"Let's do it!" Amelia said excitedly.

Amelia had laid their costumes and accessories out on the bed from head to toe like ceremonial garments. As they zipped, tied, buckled, fastened, fixed and straightened into new skins their nervous hearts beat faster.

"How do I look?" said his wife self-consciously, a slight tremble in her voice.

"Wonderful, just wonderful," replied Tom.

From his vantage point in the lime tree, after many months of cuckoo calls, and like a proud parent the Cuckoo of Awareness witnessed the riding out. The tandem passed just a few feet from him—Elvis the Captain at the front and Wonder Woman the Stoker at the back—straight into the Garden Square for a warm-up lap before heading into the more expansive territory of nearby Pittville Park, the largest ornamental park in Cheltenhamshire.

"Tom?" said a widow, walking Wongo the Wonder dog.

Tom lifted his Elvis sunglasses. "Uh-huh," he said with a hitched top lip, continuing gloriously past in full-flared, jump-suit-belted, cape billowing, side-burned, zip-up-booted, wig-wearing, hairy medallion chest magnificence.

"Amelia?" said a happily retired flasher.

"Great Hera, yes!" she replied.

"Another lap, Wonder Woman?"

"You bet, Elvis."

"Coo-Coo."

"Elvis has left the building, Cuckoo."

"From the King of the Birds to the King of Rock & Roll, I'll be quick: remember not to forget to change the identity of 'Big Bird', we don't want you incriminating the cold blooded killer that is your lovely wife!"

"I won't forget, but it will be kept up my sleeve as a marital bargaining chip."

"I would expect nothing less. Now, remember you promised me faithfully to airbrush me from existence—not that anybody will ever believe you anyway! We don't want you getting sectioned!"

"Nobody will ever get to hear of the insufferable Cuckoo of Awareness, I promise. Is that it? As you can see we are a bit pre-occupied."

"I just called in to say...I just called in to say goodbye, Tom, it's time for me to leave you now, my friend."

Tom didn't reply immediately. It took the wind out of his pedals; as he slowed down, tears filled his smiling eyes. They were tears of salvation, of gratitude. How do you thank someone for giving you something so priceless, he thought to himself. Grinning with the Presleyian answer, he spoke his last final words to his great saviour and friend.

"Thank you. Thank you very much!"

Thereafter, on that day in June at approximately the same time each year, a growing number of bikes magically appeared in the Garden of Wellington Square with costumed peddlers from all walks of life, each with a story, each pedalling, each turning their wheels, each moving, moving.

# MOOM MONSTERS (VI)

During the stay of the Moom Monsters throughout the autumn and winter months of Murria when the Wily-Wily blew, there was a favourite time of day for the Mu. It was a time that found its way into poetry and song and the hearts of the people young and old. It was at eventide, when the dark short days were drawing to a close drenching them in delicate sunset rosé wine. The children had finished their schooling and the men and women their labour on land and sea. It was in the few short hours before the Wily-Wily arrived.

The Valley of the Mu was bathed in golden Moomlight glowing from ridge to ridge above them. The Moom Monsters looked like they were scraping the sky. The Mu did not need street lighting. Imagine having the comfort of a Moom landing light. The lobster fisherman tending their pots in the bay of Murria had the best bobbing seat in the house.

The old men of Murria would meet in their favourite fireside inns to escape from the old wives of Murria. They would play games, take a drink, amuse themselves with talk, and smoke their pipes full of healthy Moom poo tobacco. The old women of Murria would do exactly the same—but with even more talking and gossiping!

Families would actually sit down to tea together as a family! Can you imagine that? These were ancient times, Freddie.

The favourite time of day was about to receive the

magic that made it a magical time of day.

The Moom were about to sing.

Not the stick your fingers in your ears singing torture that your dad dishes out in the shower. When the Moom sang everyone listened, even the birds. Angels singing would be the warm-up act before the Moom came on stage.

The Mu had a special name for the singing—Mooming.

If I open your curtains, Freddie, can you see there the brightest star glowing in the night sky? It's called Sirius. The very same brightest star the people of Murria could see also. High up on the hills in the middle of the Mooms the Mu witnessed a brighter glowing in the belly of one of the Mooms. A Sirius Moom! It had more watts than the other golden belly bulbs. This was their leader, or the Mooma, as the Mu called her. Mooma sounds similar to ma, mumma, or mother, so I am going to call her the Grand Mooma. It was not only the name that gave a clue to the sex of the Grand Mooma. She was a soprano—that meant a female singer. There was a special air of pre-concert anticipation zinging around Murria.

Due to the healthy lifestyle of the Mu there were many people well over 100 years old. In fact there were at least 100 people over 100. They remembered with warm fondness the singing that greeted the last arrival of a baby Moom to Murria. They romanticised that it was like the sound of eternity. Word quickly spread that tonight would be an exceptional evensong of Mooming to celebrate the birth of the new baby boy. Do you know, Freddie, how the Moom felt about their baby son? Exactly the same way Mummy and myself feel about you—they had a rapture in their hearts and eyes.

Twenty talking craters lined up like giant speakers to fill the cathedral of the valley with song. The speakers vibrated different voices. There were tenors, countertenors, sopranos, mezzo sopranos, baritones, basses and contraltos.

Mooming was so...I was going to say beautiful, Freddie, because I don't have a word more beautiful than beautiful to describe it. I wish I did. Just like I can't make words form a shape or put letters together that adequately describe how much I love you. If I did I would use that word to describe that love; I would also use it to describe Mooming. Perhaps the Moom created that word by turning love into song?

The universe is like a giant harp, Freddie—with strings like a spider's web—everything is connected. Mooming was an ancient duet between the Moom and the universe. The Moom knew how to play the harp—to talk with the universe—vibrating its string soul with their voices. A little bit like how your mother knows how to tickle you or stroke you to sleep. The Mu could actually hear the universe, Freddie! It was peaceful, like a comforting lullaby for children and adults. Adult's need lullabies too, not just children. The universe sounded like a warm happy memory that would sustain you forever.

All the voices would come together for the last line of each verse—the closest we have today I suppose is an Amen or Hallelujah. The Grand Mooma began playing the harp with the fingers of her high sweet solo voice, sweeter than the most accomplished opera singer, Freddie. She began and her people joined her.

We can only imagine at the beauty of their song for their newborn Moom. Some described it as like listening to the universe giving up its equations. Others compared it to reaching in and touching the warm joy of love you feel for a child inside your heart.

Sleep well, Son, I love you.

# ABOUT ATMOSPHERE PRESS

Atmosphere Press is an independent, full-service publisher for excellent books in all genres and for all audiences. Learn more about what we do at atmospherepress.com.

We encourage you to check out some of Atmosphere's latest releases, which are available at Amazon.com and via order from your local bookstore:

*The Hidden Life,* a novel by Robert Castle

*Big Beasts,* a novel by Patrick Scott

*Alvarado,* a novel by John W. Horton III

*Nothing to Get Nostalgic About*, a novel by Eddie Brophy

*GROW: A Jack and Lake Creek Book,* novel by Chris S McGee

*Home is Not This Body,* a novel by Karahn Washington

*Whose Mary Kate,* a novel by Jane Leclere Doyle

*Stuck and Drunk in Shadyside,* a novel by M. Byerly

*These Things Happen,* a novel by Chris Caldwell

*Vanity: Murder in the Name of Sin,* a novel by Rhiannon Garrard

*Blood of the True Believer,* a novel by Brandann R. Hill-Mann

*The Dark Secrets of Barth and Williams College: A Comedy in Two Semesters,* a novel by Glen Weissenberger

*The Glorious Between*, a novel by Doug Reid

*An Expectation of Plenty,* a novel by Thomas Bazar

*Sink or Swim, Brooklyn,* a novel by Ron Kemper

# ABOUT THE AUTHOR

Andrew lives in Cheltenham with his wife Sophie & 14 year old son Noah–Og 'the Dustbin Dog' & Growl Tiger the cat–resistance was futile.

He is stuck in the body of an entrepreneur but dreams of being a writer and removing the word minor that precedes poet from his biography. He is currently writing a Children's book and fearing an imminent revenge rise in his council tax following the publication of his first novel.

Lightning Source UK Ltd.
Milton Keynes UK
UKHW010813261121
394640UK00003B/400